Prague Summer

Prague Summer

a novel

JEFFREY CONDRAN

COUNTERPOINT

BERKELEY

Library of Congress Cataloging-in-Publication Data

Condran, Jeffrey.
Prague summer : a novel / Jeffrey Condran.
1. Americans—Czech Republic—Prague—Fiction. 2. Married people—
Fiction. 3. Deception—Fiction. 4. Prague (Czech Republic)—Fiction.
5. Psychological fiction. I. Title.
PS3603.O5322P73 2014
813'.6--dc23

ISBN 978-1-61902-310-9

Cover design by Ann Weinstock
Interior Design by Neuwirth & Associates

COUNTERPOINT
1919 Fifth Street
Berkeley, CA 94710
www.counterpointpress.com

Printed in the United States of America
Distributed by Publishers Group West

10 9 8 7 6 5 4 3 2 1

For Meghan and Jacob, *who love books.*

"What do we know but that we face one another in this place?"

—William Butler Yeats, "The Man and the Echo"

Prologue

The body seemed almost to float as it left the protection of the
window casement. Against the dark sky, buoyed on a humid
night's air, its pale green skirt billowed like gossamer around
thin hips and legs. The passive face of the woman looked toward
the heavens, mouth open, a few strands of dark hair caught in
the corner of her colored lips. For a moment, the whole—skirt,
legs, hips, hair—paused cinematically before remembering its
obligation to fall swiftly to the unforgiving cement below. The
back of the head and shoulders hit hard against the sidewalk
fronting the National Theatre of Prague only a half second

before the rest of the body followed. Beyond the muffled impact, not a single sound had been made.

Close by, the Vltava flowed calmly, its waters lapping in whispers against the embankment. This small splashing only accentuated the early morning quiet. Across the water, high upon the hill, the castle stood sentinel looking down on these events in the Staré Město as it had done for nearly a thousand years.

In fact, the whole of the city seemed to hold its breath, to look and watch and wait as only a city like Prague could, miraculously untouched by so much of the violence of European history, with an unending patience, dark now and sinister-seeming in its beauty. And here was the body of a young woman lying broken in its midst. Time passed: A quarter of an hour, a half, and still no one came by to notice. Finally, across the street, just by the Café Slavia, the footsteps of a woman in high heels and her male companion broke the silence. He was walking quickly, while she followed indolently behind smoking a cigarette. Occasionally, he would encourage her to hurry up, though this seemed to only slow her down more. Once she even paused to spit a flake of tobacco from her tongue. For a moment, her gaze rested upon the body of the woman, but for some reason the significance of what she saw did not register. Or perhaps she thought it simply the figure of one of the city's homeless sprawled out just where she had drunkenly fallen.

On the Masarykovo nábřeží a black Škoda flew past, kicking up a wind that briefly disturbed the loose fabric of her skirt and tossed back and forth locks of curly black hair.

It was this same wind that shifted something in the dreaming consciousness of an actual homeless man who had set up his blanket and cardboard pallet in a small, protected alcove built into the wall behind the theater, adjacent to a green dumpster. Not yet fully awake, his first move was to check his grip on a leash that held secure a sleeping puppy, not more than three months old. With some effort, the man sat up and yawned, then roughly patted the head of the dog. At once, his little tail began to thump happily against the cardboard and a pink tongue flashed out to lick the hand of his owner. After a brief stretch, man and dog walked behind the dumpster and, unzipping his fly, the man relieved himself long and noisily upon the ground. He took a deep breath, too deep perhaps, because he coughed. Still, waking with his new puppy in the quiet of the early morning—having the whole of the world to himself, no fuss, no hassles, not even (if only briefly) any unnatural cravings—was his favorite part of the day.

For a moment as he clumsily adjusted his fly, his vigilance faltered and the leash fell from his hand. Immediately the puppy began to trot away to explore. The dumpster, of course, was well known to him. He heard his owner's call and knew that sooner than later he would heed that friendly voice and come trotting back, but first there were so many good smells to investigate. Bird droppings, empurpled from ripe berries, presented themselves to be gobbled up, a dollop of creamy mustard dropped from a tourist's sausage, perhaps a little crusted over but still delicious, and then something new carried on the wind and just around the corner of the building.

"Arno!" the man called. But the puppy had already moved out of sight and the man was running after him as quickly as his stiff legs could go. At first, he thought that the dog was worrying the end of a rolled carpet—at least, that's the story he told to the Policie. But then he saw the hair blowing, the legs bent beneath the figure at an unnatural angle, and one black pump securely gripped in his puppy's teeth.

"Oh, shit!" he wailed and ran very fast indeed to close the distance between himself and the dog before any further damage could be done. His voice was horrible and strangled as he yelled at the dog, scaring him. "Get away, get away! Get away from that thing!"

One

Selma Al-Khateeb is coming to stay with us in Prague.

"I should have asked you first, I know," Stephanie says, exaggerating the *I know*, zooming her words in a way that's supposed to make me laugh. It's my wife's idea of being charming. "You don't mind, do you?"

"No," I say, "your friend needs you."

Three twentysomethings wearing nothing but jockstraps and curly neon-green wigs have walked with a large posse of followers onto Masarykovo nábřeží and are blocking traffic. They are swaying in circles and barking laughter at each other. The limousine driver fumes silently, but his hands betray his frustration, the fingers curling and jerking in angry gestures above the wheel of the Mercedes.

"Still, we have to try to act as normal as possible," Stephanie says. "She's not sick, no one has died."

"Not yet," I say, to which Stephanie gives me The Look.

Out the window I can see two Policie running with one hand on their caps to keep them from flying away. They pass a beggar, almost unnoticed, who has set himself up on the sidewalk. I have a deep sympathy for the beggars of Prague. They are so unlike the cup-jingling hustlers you see in New York or Washington. No, this man has a decorum, a gravitas, that never fails to impress me. His hair is buzzed short, and his clothes, though shabby, are neat and worn smartly. But what has never quite stopped surprising me is his posture: The man crouches nearly prostrate on the ground, almost like a Muslim at prayer, his forehead resting on the pavement, his hands out before him in supplication. He speaks to no one, silent, his needs absolutely clear.

I turn to Stephanie in order to point him out to her, to say for the fiftieth time how moved I am by these beggars, but I can see immediately that she is too engrossed with the subject of Selma's arrival to pay any real attention.

"What are her plans?" I say to be polite. Even though we've been married for ten years, or maybe *because* we've been married for so long, I find it increasingly satisfying to be as polite as possible to my wife.

"I don't think she has any—*not yet*." Stephanie smiles. I am forgiven.

All of my wife's close friends, a tight circle—a witch's coven,

I joke—are worried about Selma and her husband. She's smiling now, but even a quick glance at Stephanie's fingers reveals the damage of her anxiety. I'd love to change the subject. Today is my wife's birthday, it's late June in the most beautiful city in the world, and I want her to have a good time.

Nevertheless, I say, "Maybe we should find something for her to do?"

She loops her arm with mine and leans across me to get a better look out the window. The crowds of tourists around the Charles Bridge are tightly packed. It's a sight we've seen a million times, as normal as breathing. I return to Stephanie. She is pale skinned and dark haired. Crow's-feet have begun to establish themselves around her eyes. I have just given her a diamond necklace that I paid more money for than I have for anything in my life except cars and apartments. Not even my first edition of *The Sheltering Sky* cost quite as much. I smile because she can't stop touching it, afraid that somehow the necklace will have disappeared between one moment and the next. A sweet aroma rises from her long hair, and I wonder if she realizes how attracted to her I continue to be.

After enjoying her for a moment, I try to follow her gaze out the window. The absolute lack of movement in the traffic seems to have everyone on edge. In the car beside us, a long and stately '90s-era Mercedes, a man who is just beginning to be old is having a heated argument with his wife. I think he looks like a classical musician, his white hair deeply receding but thick and full on the sides like lush wings. He, too, is gesturing toward the green-wigged crowd, explaining to his wife, who is very thin and fussy-looking, that there is no way to have anticipated this kind of delay. I pretend they are headed to the National Theatre where I know *Othello* is playing. Beside me, Stephanie sighs. She has seen them, too.

We used to play this game together all the time, imagining the lives of strangers. It was a kind of competition, mildly serious but mostly fun. We could do it now, I think, but again decide to let it go. Some deep domestic instinct keeps me quiet. Instead, I smile to encourage her to answer my question.

"She can't work," Stephanie says. "It would take forever to arrange the paperwork. Besides, I don't think that's what she has in mind."

"I thought you said you didn't know her plans."

"Well," she says, "I don't. Not really."

Finally, the driver can't take it any longer. He opens his window and sticks out his head and shoulders. He swears at the young people in the streets, at the police, no doubt at life. His Czech is so fast I can't make out all of it. Something like, "Sons of a diseased pig!" I'm not sure, but it makes Stephanie laugh.

She turns to me, still smiling. "Let's just see what happens."

"Who are these lunatics?" I say.

"*Stag!*" the driver bellows. "*Stag! Stag!*" He gestures, palms up in exasperation, and I laugh. To me he is also a part of the wonderful circus that is Prague with his graying bowl cut and bristly sideburns and cigarette smell. A Czech George Harrison. If he were a cabdriver, I'd be wondering if I would have to wrangle with him over the fare.

"Staying with us is meant to be an *escape* for Selma."

"We're going to be good to her and kind to her," I say. "That's something we can do. But she's not likely to forget her husband's been arrested by the FBI."

"Of course she's not going to forget," Stephanie says. She squeezes her eyes shut and massages her temples. "But Mansour is innocent. I want her to be surrounded by people who believe that. Absolutely."

"I'm not sure I believe anything absolutely."

"Maybe I don't care what you believe," she says. "I just need your help."

Ah, my help. Selma has mentioned in at least one email that while she's here she wants to see literary Prague. This is about the only thing I've been allowed to know. She wants to see the house where Kafka lived; the Café Slavia, where all the '60s writers and intellectuals drank their coffee and slivovitz; and perhaps even make a foray or two into the contemporary scene. Selma's bachelor's degree was in English Literature, so as they say, she has an interest. And I suppose this is what I had in mind when I said that we should find something for her to do.

"We'll do everything we can for her," I say. "Full effort. A hundred percent."

"This is why you're my favorite husband," she says, and I get a little kiss on the cheek.

Quarrel averted. Peace restored.

"How long can it possibly take to round up a stag party?" she says.

"Sometimes I think the Czechs actually stage little moments like this."

"So we can have a good story to tell at the party?"

"Side benefit," I say, "but true."

"And people say History has ended in the Czech Republic."

Finally the police have restored some semblance of order and Masarykovo nábřeží is nearly cleared. There, just in front of a shop selling handcrafted wooden puppets, the stag party has been gathered and handcuffed. One young man's wig has gone terribly askew, covering his left eye. With his hands restrained, he cannot adjust it. He is wearing a pair of huge bug-eye sunglasses. His legs are thin and his skin is the palest shade of white. A clump of wiry black hair sprouts from the center of his chest. Beside him, one of his comrades has his back to traffic, his pathetic little dimpled butt hanging out for all to see. I am suddenly thrilled to be part of a generation that is mercifully not obsessed with photographing everything.

"Gross," Stephanie says.

Life in Prague, it seems, is 40 percent composed of living down embarrassment of your fellow countrymen. How does one explain to the locals green wigs and jockstraps? One does not.

"I've decided that stag parties are operating on the 'Don't shit where you live' philosophy," I say. "Save all your hooligan impulses for Prague."

"What happens in Prague stays in Prague," Stephanie says.

Whole vacations planned around the single premise of drunken insanity. Like Spring Break: Europe. I'm waiting for the reality show. No wonder the driver thinks we're pigs. Or sons of pigs. With a disease. Isn't it only monsters that have happily thrown away all sense of shame?

"If it makes you feel any better," I quip, "with butts like those, I'd say it's likely those particular boys are British."

"It's a consolation," Stephanie says. "But God, I'm imagining their hangovers."

"I'm imagining waking up in a Czech jail wearing nothing but a jockstrap."

And then we laugh, and the moment is a good one. This is what marriage is like when it's going well—a shared sense of absurdity. To laugh together until you cry. And then laugh again. Now I know that, barring something unforeseen, Stephanie will have a good time at the party and we will inch closer to Selma's arrival in a state of general simpatico.

"Idiots!" the driver says.

"Absolutely," we say together.

Secretly, though, I am glad the stag parties are here, part of Prague. Isn't this the kind of thing I came to find? The green wigs, the cab drivers, the bumbling and corrupt police, the throngs of humanity, the stink of traffic, the promise of a party, all played out on a stage so spectacular that it can absorb almost anything, like the ocean, and still preserve its beauty.

In a moment the street is clear and the traffic is moving. I can feel the thrum of the limo's engine. The whole episode is already becoming a memory. I catch a glimpse of the bridge towers and a statue on the north side of the entrance to Charles Bridge, *The Madonna Attending to St. Bernard*. Again, I think to point it out to Stephanie, but we are moving too swiftly and the moment is gone, and so are we, finally, into the summer night, ready to begin.

The door of the Globe Bookstore & Café is opened by a waiter in black, a Czech, and the elegant front room is revealed before us. Wooden shelving filled with English-language books, a couple of well-placed chairs, tables lined with the latest arrivals, and best of all, a spiral staircase leading up to a second-floor balcony with more shelving and more books. The space, however, is dominated by a tall counter where the cash register is placed and where there are stacks of fliers and brochures advertising everything from rooms for rent to guitar lessons to the monthly meeting of a local literary book club that calls itself The Inklings. I am a member.

The bookstore is closed; this is a private party hosted by the owners, Michael Leo and his wife, Anna Nemcova. They are the ones who ordered the limousine. *Děkuji.* Their lives, I have said to Stephanie, are the epicenter of the world. But I am biased. In moments, we are given drinks. Sangria served in champagne flutes. In her glass, a bit of orange.

"There is Maria Fuentes, the Venezuelan poet," our friend Anthony whispers.

She is blind, or nearly so. Apparently she can see shapes and gradations of light. When she's speaking to you her dead eyes are always just a little bit off the mark, like a woman who is already thinking beyond the conversation she's having with you to the next, clearly more engaging one. But I have heard her recite her poems and her voice is rich and honeyed. She closes her eyes as she's reciting and I imagine her seeing the lines, one by one, flashing along the white screen of her consciousness.

She has wonderfully wide hips. When she moves, I have to stop myself from following her around the room.

Now Anthony is pointing out Kara Mullins, an American from Washington whose father is the CEO of an insurance company and who sold her apartment in the Watergate Building to open a restaurant in the Staré Město. We have eaten there. Not a single pork dish on the menu, not a potato dumpling in sight. There are musicians, writers, students from Charles University. Americans, Irish, Germans, Australians, Spanish, even a few Czechs. One can meet everybody here.

"There is Luke Nevin."

"Who is he?" Stephanie asks.

Nevin is an independent filmmaker. He is thin, his skinny jeans showing off the S-curve of his hips. Curly hair. Big, black-rimmed glasses, like the 1950s on steroids. His first short film was nominated for an Academy Award. He is as gay, Anthony says, as the day is long. Women surround him.

"Have you seen his film?"

Michael has joined us. "Endlessly," he says. "It's in black and white. Twenty-four minutes of Millennial Generation love. Anna says she contracted chlamydia just from watching."

We can hear Luke Nevin's voice. It is clear and sweet sounding but peppered with those signature "like, like, likes" that render all of life into the conditional.

"I talked to her last night and, *like*, she was so, *like*, pulling a diva snit on me . . . " he says.

As fate would have it—or perhaps it was planned?—Nevin is standing in front of a shelf of books dedicated to gay and lesbian erotica. A Mapplethorpe coffee-table book is visible just behind the dark cloud of his hair.

" . . . Yes, yes, yes, she's *going* to do it. I don't care."

Out of nowhere, a cake materializes. It is chocolate with raspberry preserves baked into it, raspberry icing. On the sides are chocolate-dipped wafers, girded around with a red ribbon. On top of the cake it reads, *Št'astné narozeniny, Stephanie!* Everyone sings. She is both touched and embarrassed—perfect.

Michael and I arranged the cake together. He has been in Prague since the beginning—meaning since 1990. Graying hair that he still styles spiked up in the front like a frat boy. Expensive shirts. The weight of experience lending an authority that feels absolute. He is our Gertrude Stein but without the sexual politics or annoying repetitions. A drink is a drink is a drink. The first time I met him was during the European soccer championships. I was watching in the Globe's café, the broadcast projected from a laptop onto a wall that had been cleared of paintings and photographs. The room was filled with Italians and Spaniards and Germans. Michael's wife bought me my first *Beton*. Anna is spectacular, a body double for Paulina Porizkova. Long straight hair, a pert little ass, legs so long and thin the insides of her thighs have never touched. She is perhaps now forty-five. Some nights I imagine her at twenty but can't stay with it. The knowledge is too painful, a thing that burns the mind, like reading the First Language before Babel. She is from Brno, the hometown of Milan Kundera. Her one fault is that she tells this to every new person she meets.

Anthony has wandered over to talk to her. He is, for me, like a character out of a novel. Jake Barnes without the unfortunate injury. He writes for the *Prague Post*. There are nearly fifty thousand Americans in the city and everyone reads it. God knows what he might be saying to Anna. They like to pretend to be lascivious together, but it is just a game for them. In their private dialogues everyone is an adulterer, everyone's pussy smells, everyone fingerpaints on their lover's stomach in menstrual blood. My wife has to be very drunk to appreciate them.

To break away from these ideas I wander alone behind the bar of the café. I am attracted to the bottles of alcohol. The shape of the glass, the labels, the soft light reflecting from the surfaces. Johnnie Walker Red, Becherovka, Bombay Sapphire. On and on, row after row, like old friends waiting in line. On the end of the bar itself is the espresso machine. It's easy to imagine Michael and Anna here in the early morning, the smell of strong coffee in the air, the wordless comfort of their marriage. She is turning the pages of the newspaper. After a while he will switch on the radio to the classical music station. Half a grapefruit on each spouse's plate. Chocolate brioche. A cherished quietude before the staff arrives, before they must become Michael Leo and Anna Nemcova.

Anna has found me.

"Why are you all alone in here?" she says.

"I was admiring the bar."

"It's beautiful," she says. "We are alike, Henry. I have decided that this is the case. Like you, I find that in every party there is a moment when it's best to be alone. And so, we find ourselves together. Ironical, no?"

I smile.

One of the waitresses joins us at the bar with a tray full of dirty glasses. "Have you met, Holly? She is our latest hire. She is so beautiful. Don't you think she's beautiful?"

Holly is, indeed, lovely. She has an intelligent face and the most perfect posture I think I have ever seen. She is Australian and doing her travel year. Anna and I argue about what it's called. Roundabout. Walkabout. Holly doesn't bother to correct either of us. Astute.

From the bookstore, I can hear other guests arriving. Holly wants to hurry back to the action but Anna is determined to introduce us.

"Holly must know you," she says.

I wonder if Anna is already drunk. And I'm concerned that she thinks I'll have any interest in an eighteen-year-old Australian—or that Holly will have any interest in me. It strikes me as one of Anna's games. For the moment, it's probably best to play. "Holly, this is Henry Marten. The tenth most interesting man in Prague. Henry loves books, he's a dealer, so you won't be able to afford anything." Anna laughs and laughs and laughs at her own joke. "Tell her the name of your shop, Henry."

"Hades Rare Books."

"And the rest of it, the rest of it."

"Hades Rare Books: *Help Save an Old Book from the Underworld.*" I give Holly a business card. "Come by someday. I'll find something you can buy."

Holly, of course, loves books. That's why she's working at the Globe.

"Tell him your real ambition."

Holly wants to be a writer.

Anna puts her hand on the girl's arm. "Tell him your favorite writer."

"Does there have to be just one?" Holly says.

"No," I say.

"I love Dostoevsky," Anna says, pronouncing the name with the thickest Russian accent she can muster.

Holly and I agree to the excellence of Dostoevsky.

"I love *The Unbearable Lightness of Being*," Holly says. "That book is why I came to Prague."

"That's a better reason than most," I say.

"You love Milan Kundera? Oh, Holly. Did you know that he is from Brno?" Anna says. "That is so significant. I am from Brno, too!"

And off we go. But something has opened up in my mind about Holly. A whole new psychological complexity. I imagine her lying in her bedroom back in Sydney or Melbourne or wherever, a paperback clutched in her hands, her brow creased in concentration, trying to untie the knots of Nietzschean philosophy, Freudian sexuality, Soviet communism, the paradoxical nature of existence. Coupled with her perfect posture, it would be easy to be a little bit in love with Holly from Australia.

"Look at his face," Anna says, laughing. "You've won him over. Milan Kundera is his hero."

Holly laughs and blushes and, just in that moment, we see my wife standing in the doorway.

———

In the limousine on the way home: "Don't you dare fuck that little Australian bitch."

"She's a waitress."

"Don't-do-it."

"I won't."

"You better not."

The castle floats by on the hill above us. Lit softly from below, it looks like a fairy-tale world. A place where even jealousy can be made romantic.

"Why don't you fuck me instead?" I say softly. Stephanie rolls her eyes.

"Why don't you go fuck yourself?" she says. But there's a little smile on her lips as she says it. She doesn't want me to see.

Rule Number 1 of a Successful Marriage: *Always be prepared to make a fool of yourself.*

———

In bed, Stephanie wears the pink pajamas that her mother sent her from Baltimore. My mother-in-law has excellent taste, as the thin fabric clings to Stephanie's body in the most pleasant ways. I am happy to watch her run little errands around the bedroom: putting on her glasses now that the contacts are in their case by the bathroom sink, slathering her legs in pomegranate-scented body butter, talking to our cat, Cheerio, in a baby voice, plugging her cell phone into its charger. All these little moves are made even pleasanter by the fact that I'm happily drunk on sangria and *Betons*. We like to watch a single episode of *Poirot* each night, but often, after parties, we skip it and go straight to bed. Stephanie and I are both addicted to Agatha Christie's Belgian detective. It's a loss to us when we don't end the day with him.

"What about Poirot?" Stephanie says, getting under the covers. Somehow her toes are cold even in the summertime.

I put on my own glasses to look at the clock. "It's quarter to one."

"Ugh, that's late."

"Fuck it. Let's watch one."

Stephanie claps her hands in delight, as if she had needed my permission to stay up late to watch TV on a Saturday night.

"Which episode?"

"Pick it."

In a few minutes the DVD is humming along in the machine and the opening credits are flashing across the screen. If there were words to the theme music, I swear we'd lie there and sing along. David Suchet makes his first appearance with Hugh Fraser as Hastings. The scene is set in the detective's London apartment, a 1930s modernist fantasy with every knickknack perfectly placed to assuage Poirot's OCD.

"I wish our apartment looked like that," Stephanie says.

"No you don't."

"I do."

"You'd hate it if you actually had to live with that furniture."

"You're probably right."

"I remember this one," I say.

"We've seen them all four times."

"I know, I'm just saying that I remember it."

"News flash."

We are lying on our sides, snuggled together, my wife's soft bum nestled against my lap. Almost unconsciously, I begin to gently rub it under the covers.

"Is this the one where Poirot says, 'I have never met the corpse whose heart still beats'?"

"No, that's another one."

"Really."

"Umm-hmm."

As the episode goes on and Poirot begins his unraveling of the crime, Stephanie wiggles closer, moving the muscles of her bottom in infinitesimal little contractions. She is teasing me. I kiss her hair.

"Wait for it," she says.

Finally, Poirot completes his demonstration of *the little gray cells* and I am free to have my wife. I grab a handful of her hair and move it away from the back of her neck and kiss her there. Stephanie giggles like we haven't done this a thousand times, and I think to myself, wonderingly, that it feels so good to actually be in love with your wife. As if this were a novel idea, as if I had actually invented it. Despite this good feeling, I know there are only a few ways that this will play out. We have a repertoire honed down over the years, finely tested from an initial, much broader pool of variables. Sex with Stephanie is not the best I have ever experienced. But those other connections, while vivid and intense, were sprints. Stephanie is a marathon. And so, perhaps naturally, there are restrictions. While I might wish that these were not in place, there are pleasures here to following the rules, to winning a game that has, let's not call them limits, but traditions. Think of chess. There are a finite number of pieces, they may only move in certain ways, and yet to contrive victory from them is a distinct pleasure.

She turns to face me and I kiss the end of her jawline, just by the ear, because her skin tastes so clean and fresh there and because she loves it. Eventually, I will flick my tongue on the back of her earlobe and, when I do, she arches her back. A signal sent, a message received. When I kiss my way down to the soft skin of her belly, she lifts the pajama shirt over her head and lies back against the pillow. My fingers walk slowly over her breasts and neck until I tangle them among the diamonds of the necklace. I give a gentle tug. Wearing the necklace without her top makes her look especially naked. I drink in the sight of her breasts and skin, the almost V of her upturned chin—I had anticipated this little picture from the moment I laid eyes on the necklace in the jewelry store. Then, unexpectedly, a quick vision of Holly intrudes. Her long straight back, her firm ass. I put the waistband of Stephanie's pajama bottoms between my teeth in order to chase it away. Go, Holly. You've caused enough trouble.

Her body has lost just a touch of, well, what would Henry Miller call it? *Juice.* Some of the body's freshness has slowly dissipated, but the shape of her is the same as it's always been. Beautiful. I'm no critic. There's not an ounce of judgment there. How could there be? It is another courtesy we perform for each other: no judgments. Observations are fine. So are little jokes. But no judgments. My own body couldn't stand up to her critical eye. The rounding of my belly, the gray materializing in my dark hair. I haven't let myself go, but I'm no longer the man she married.

And so it goes—not at all unhappily. Birthday sex accomplished.

———————

Stephanie is almost immediately asleep. I, on the other hand, am still too drunk. It's the Becherovka, an alcohol much like gin, and mixed with tonic it becomes a *Beton*. It is *my* drink, in the same way that Camel Lights Hard Pack used to be my brand of cigarettes when it was still cool to smoke, and the way I drink my coffee the same every morning: French press, black, two sugars. It is a silly way to make a life, but there you are. Again, I have had too much to drink and my body won't let me settle. Every time I put my head on the pillow I can feel my heart beating and the tops of my ears are hot. For an hour, I try to lie there with Stephanie, an act of solidarity that I know she appreciates, but ultimately there's nothing to do but get up.

It's a warm night, and suddenly, a remnant of my thought about Henry Miller still rattling around in my head, I decide that I want to take a walk. In the dark, I put on an old pair of jeans and a navy blue T-shirt, sandals, and go out into the night. There is a half moon and a gentle breeze. As I stand in front of the door of our apartment building, I think what a joke it is to compare myself to Miller. All those descriptions of walking the streets of Paris at night, homeless, furtively picking up cigarette butts, and getting erections from looking at the statues in the Jardin des Tuileries. There is a line that always stays with me: "I have no money, no resources, no hopes. I am the happiest man alive." Henry Miller was poor. And if I am not exactly rich, no one on this Earth would ever call me poor. We are not yet forty years old, but we own a three-bedroom apartment in the Jewish Quarter of Prague, garage a late-model Volkswagen, and lease a storefront in the Mala Strana for the bookshop. Still, at almost two in the morning, in the dark of a June night in a foreign city, postcoital and still a little drunk, it's possible for such disparities to be overlooked and for me to channel the ghost of one of my literary heroes.

I am an American in Europe, after all. Even if Miller would condemn me to being Henry James.

Just down the street is my favorite place in all the world: the Café Franz Kafka. It is closed at this hour, the lights off, its short awning flapping gently. Like the *Betons*, this is *my café*. Stephanie and I have a drink here almost every evening. I meet clients here. I practice my Czech on the bartenders. They know me. I waste hour after hour here some days, a book in hand, almost no regrets. Across the street and down a little is a statue of Kafka himself. Tourists stop to take their picture beside it. I reach up now and pat the statue's shoulder.

So close, it feels like an obligation to make a stop at the Jewish Cemetery. The space, behind a black iron fence, is small, the headstones jutting out of the soft earth like crooked teeth. The Jews have buried their dead in layers here, one generation on top of the other, so that slowly, the ground shifts or erupts here and there to displace a stone. I cannot imagine some kind of cosmic orthodontist coming along to straighten them. I am not Jewish, but I have been very close to one or two, and the place feels sacred to me, especially at night. Once, I climbed the fence in order to find the headstone of Rabbi Judah Loew ben Bezalel, the man who is supposed to have conjured up the Golem from the clay of the Vltava. That night I had an empty chocolate tin with me, about the size of my hand, and I filled it with dirt from beside the rabbi's grave. It is kept on my desk at the bookshop.

I move on. The night is quiet, and no one passes close to me—though in a city like Prague it is impossible to ever truly be alone. Soon I discover myself passing the shops on Paris Avenue. I am headed toward the river. I did not know it at first, but I know it now. I take a deep breath. The world seems timeless. My heart has stopped pounding and it is clear that I will live forever.

More quickly than I thought possible I am by the Rudolfinum Conservatory, a building that the Nazis took over and made their headquarters in Prague. I have always wished the place were quieter, not so close to the traffic. But so much is preserved in Prague that it doesn't seem right to complain.

I feel alive, happy. I almost want another drink.

There is a short flight of stairs that lead down to the river walk. I take them slowly, one of my knees a little gimpy. This *was* my destination. The water moving quietly beside me, a liquid black that feels like it could contain anything—and probably does. On the river walk there are more people. Couples with their arms thrown around each other, old men smoking cigarettes, tourists, even at two in the morning, taking photographs of the bridge and the castle. Who could blame them? I am smiling, relaxed. My heart is open. I think to myself that I am even ready to welcome my wife's friend, Selma Al-Khateeb, for as long as she likes. Two months, six months, it doesn't matter. So long as I get to keep selling my books, drinking with my friends, and making love to my wife. So long as there isn't another revolution and I'm not sent back to New York. So long as I can stay in this place forever, I can be content.

Prosím.

Two

The café table looks out onto Široká ulice, which is bathed in early summer sunlight, the air warm and clean feeling, not an ounce of humidity in the Prague morning. Already the streets are filling up with people, the German tourists being the earliest risers. The statue of Kafka stands sentinel across the street and I sit with a large bowl of coffee and an elaborate brochure for a new exhibit of rare books on display at the New Town Hall in the Nové Město. I am just wondering about Stephanie when she walks through the door and plunks herself down across from me.

She does not like to talk until she's had coffee. I signal to the waitress and Stephanie and I sit together quietly until it arrives, steam rising from the bowl in twisting, pleasant waves. I like my wife especially on Sunday mornings. Sleepy, makeup-free, a stillness and self-possession that elude her on most other days. Stephanie has a Dr. Jekyll and Mr. Hyde personality. At home with me: sweet, almost girly, mildly insecure. At the embassy: competent, decisive, and watch-out-tougher-than-she-looks. In fact, I think, looking at the clean skin pulled tight around her eyes, her personality is far more complex than that. So many masks, so many little nuances. I find her endlessly fascinating.

A cell phone rings and we start digging in pockets and purses. We have the same phone, same ringtone. Ridiculous. This time, it's mine.

"Hi, Michael," I say for Stephanie's benefit. She nods and smiles, waves at the phone so that I'll say hello for her.

"Goddamn, Anna just told me what happened," he says. "Please say it didn't ruin her night."

"All's well. She had a great time."

"Oh, thank God," he says. "Now I don't have to fire Holly."

"No, don't fire anybody. But I have to say, Maria Fuentes dedicating her reading to Stephanie was a nice touch."

"Wasn't it?" Michael laughs at himself, at his own charm and charisma, at the wonderfulness of his life. Once again he's had a good time and avoided trouble. "Are we still on for this afternoon?"

"I think so," I say. "But with the party, I haven't had a chance to run it by Stephanie. Hold on."

My wife, a few sips of coffee in her, has picked up the brochure and is flipping through it.

"There's an exhibition of rare—" I begin, but she cuts me off.

"Yes," she says. "Go. It's fine. And no, I don't want to come along."

"We're on," I say to Michael.

Stephanie shakes her head and smiles. Then she drops the brochure onto the table and turns her attention to people-watching on the street. She holds the coffee reverently with both hands.

"Should we have lunch before we go?" Michael says.

"Absolutely. Where do you think?"

"Karluv Hostinec? Restaurace U Pinkasu?"

"U Pinkasu. I'm feeling traditional."

"I'll pick you up," Michael says.

"I'm at the Franz Kafka."

"Perfect."

I hang up and toss the phone on top of the brochure. Stretch. Take a deep breath. Then another sip of coffee. I join Stephanie in people-watching.

"Michael's picking me up," I say.

"What's Michael's angle?" Stephanie asks.

"What do you mean?"

"This isn't business for him. The Globe only sells new books."

"Nothing is for sale," I say. "I think he just wants to hang out."

It's a little disappointing, but we both understand what she's insinuating: Michael rarely does anything that doesn't clearly advantage him in some way. Michael does not tag along, almost never artlessly *hangs out*. It doesn't have to be devious, but Stephanie's probably right—something will most assuredly come up.

"A hundred crowns says it has something to do with Anna," Stephanie says. "She was awfully drunk last night."

At this moment we have that long-married-couple-collusion thing going, an almost Wonder Twins' Power *Activate!* moment, where all of our strength resides in the deep and abiding connection we have with each other. For the first time this morning, my wife's eyes are clear, and she's sitting up straight, ready to ferret out the juicy gossip of Michael Leo's and Anna Nemcova's lives. If Stephanie had a tail, she'd be wagging it.

"If he's looking for a favor," I say, "I wonder what it has to do with me."

"Meaning you don't think of yourself as a person who could render Michael Leo a favor."

"Something like that."

"Who knows?" Stephanie says. "You may underestimate your place in his life."

"What does that mean?"

"Nothing *lascivious*. Don't worry."

"The guy has a thousand friends," I say.

"Name one friend of Michael's who you think would do something for him purely out of friendship rather than what they thought it would do for them."

"Me."

"I rest my case."

"Possibly."

"You guys are having lunch first? At U Pinkasu?"

"Yes."

"That's when he'll hit you with it. You'll be drinking Pilsner. Three or four sips into the second beer, that's when he'll do it."

"What are you now? Nostradamus?"

"You heard it here first. Second beer."

We both sip our coffee for a few minutes and I try to imagine what Michael might have on his mind. It's intriguing, but nothing I'm troubled by. We are literary friends, that's all. That's enough.

"If it's something about Anna, I can't imagine what the favor could be. There's no way, and I mean no way that he's going to be soliciting marriage advice from me."

"You never know."

I think for a minute about Anna Nemcova. A Czech. A member of the generation who jingled their keys and brought down the Communists shouting, "Havel to the castle," part of a people who elected a writer as the president of their nation. A woman who studied poetry at the New School, who seemed to have an endless supply of family money, and who, almost twenty years ago now, married the hippest American in Prague. Michael Leo, who had spoken his horribly accented Czech with such perfect confidence. A man whose bookstore and café had been written about in travel guides, in magazines, and who famously made a perfect *Beton* for Rick Steves.

"I hope they're not getting divorced," Stephanie says.

"What?"

"Michael and Anna," she says. "I hope they're not getting a divorce."

"God forbid," I say. "It would be the end of an era."

"Chances are it's something else."

"God, now you've put the idea in my head."

It would, of course, be horrible if my friend's marriage were at an end—but I am being entirely selfish. Last night and this morning, I have been basking in contentment, thinking my life perfect, thinking—if I'm really being honest with myself—that I have finally found a home. Maybe it's silly, but Michael and Anna are a big part of the city to me, of what it represents. If something should happen to them, what else might fail in such a fragile ecosystem?

I check the time on my phone. "Michael will be here soon," I say. "Let's talk about something else."

But we do not. Instead we fall quiet, sitting together more or less comfortably in our favorite café, waiting for Michael to pick me up. I often believe that this is what life really consists of, these quiet, seemingly unremarkable moments. A stretch of minutes where our breathing is unconscious, our minds engaged but essentially at rest, no striving, no real machinating. I'm worried in a vague way about my friend, but I'm not hatching any schemes, not formulating some intervention. I look absently through the brochure in front of me. I push my foot against my wife's under the table and she pushes back. I watch a group of Americans snapping photos of the buildings with their cell phones.

Still, on the edge of all this, something new has been

introduced. It is not necessarily a bad feeling. More like a portentousness. Michael is coming. Selma, too.

I had never expected to know someone who knew someone who had been arrested by the FBI. I have never met Selma's husband, Mansour, but I have seen pictures. He is short, slight — harmless looking. He wears little round eyeglasses. Over the last few days I have imagined men in gray suits planting GPS markers underneath his car, photographing the front of his apartment building, surreptitiously interviewing the people he works with, finally breaking down his front door in the middle of the night and dragging him away. I have no idea if any of this is even the slightest bit true. I suppose we will soon know. That the circumstances of his arrest are not common knowledge probably demonstrates an admirable restraint in Selma. Imagine: our friend, a martyr to the War on Terror.

It's enough to give a person pause. It's not as if people don't think about these things in Prague. Weren't the early stages of the 9/11 cell, or was it the Underground bombing, organized here? I feel sure I read about that somewhere. And, of course, everybody knows about the Russian mafia, the Bulgarian mafia, the mafia's mafia. Fuck. What I mean is that Prague feels like an open city. What couldn't happen here? What hasn't already happened here? Perhaps Stephanie had it wrong, perhaps History has not ended in the Czech Republic.

"What are you thinking about?" Stephanie asks.

"Why?"

"You've just had the oddest expression on your face."

"Oh," I say, laughing a little.

"I was thinking about Selma."

"We should probably take her out to dinner on her first night."

"Sounds wonderful."

Michael would tell me I've read too many novels, which is true. I decided—God knows when—that most of what's reported about Muslim terrorism is hyperbole, a perverse entertainment, like reporting murders on the six o'clock news back in Pittsburgh or Minneapolis or San Jose, an excuse for newscasters to employ a dramatic timbre to their voices, a way to make us grateful for what we've got instead of looking too closely at what we do not. It's an old, old game. I tell myself repeatedly that I have moved to Prague because I no longer want to play.

"Maybe we could take her on the river?" Stephanie says.

"The food is always so horrible on those cruises."

"We could eat somewhere else beforehand."

I love my wife. This is her friend, and nothing worries her. And if a representative of the United States government isn't concerned, why should I be?

"Let's put it down as a possibility."

"Done."

———

At just a few minutes after noon, Michael roars up outside the Franz Kafka in his new Jaguar XK convertible. The color of the car is platinum with a kind of pearlescent glow. Michael is dressed in jeans and a snow-white shirt and navy blazer. His eyes are hidden behind old-style Wayfarers. He looks classic, the idol of his generation. Where have I read that? Somewhere good, a writer I like. It will come to me later, long after the moment has passed. He and I seem to wear the same uniform— today we have the same jeans, though my jacket is camel colored with darker patches at the elbow—but he seems to wear his with a whole other degree of style.

When I take my place in the passenger seat, my body feels encased in the high-grade ergonomics of the leather, like being held in the palm of a gloved hand. Thank God I will never have to drive such a car. The dual responsibilities of driving as fast as possible and yet not running down pedestrians would be too much for me. I even feel vaguely uncomfortable just sitting here in the passenger seat with nothing to do but look around. Which is just what I do. Prague, from behind the wheel of a speeding Jaguar, is nothing but a series of bright sunlight colors, the faint impression of people on the street looking back at me with envy in their eyes, and the fluid geometric shapes of the buildings. Michael always seems to be laughing when he drives, his white teeth bared, an ironic snarl ready, I think, to emanate at any moment from some deep place at the back of his throat, though I cannot help but wonder whether or not those same teeth are mired with bugs at the end of a drive. He has U2's "Beautiful Day" blaring from the CD player. His fingers tap on the wheel, his toes on the floor mat. Between the music and the wind it's impossible to speak to each other. Michael simply points at things he wants me to notice with the index finger of his right hand: a Roma cradling a black lab puppy, a tall African on stilts wearing a long red coat and black top hat, one beautiful woman after another. It's easy with this man, in this car, in this city, to forget almost everything that's supposed to be on your mind, to live just as the Buddhists want us to— entirely in the moment. Between tracks on the CD I hear a man shouting, in English, "How could you *forget* her name day? It's her *fucking* name day, you stupid fucking idiot!"

It takes us longer to find a parking space by the restaurant than it did to drive here.

It's possible now to actually look at Michael. He is engineering the best table he can find—by a window, close enough to other people to be seen, far enough away not to be overheard, a certain congenial distance from the bar and, of course, nowhere near the door to the kitchen. All of this as I admire the rough plaster of the restaurant's interior, the wrought-iron accents, the dramatic arch that separates the entry from the dining room. Tiny oil lamps are on every table, and paintings of contemporary Czech and German artists adorn the walls. We have eaten here many times before, and yet when we sit down across from each other, Michael smiles and shrugs his shoulders and raises his palms in the air faux dramatically, as if he's offering the restaurant to me. It could be the interior of any three-star restaurant in Europe, but the food is pure Czech traditional: pork in six different ways, goulash, potato dumplings, hardly a green vegetable in sight. We are only a few blocks away from the exhibit at the New Town Hall.

"They're doing something right here," Michael says. He's pleased with himself again; Michael is always pleased with himself.

"It feels good in here," I agree.

"Yes," Michael says. "That's one of the reasons we're friends, Henry. Not very many men are sensitive to these things, to the emotional resonances of spaces."

"You mean not many *straight* men."

"Ha! Yes, well, not many straight *American* men."

Where does one get such confidence? Is it possible to be born with it? His story is not that of some old-money East Coast scion who prepped at the right schools and went to Yale on a legacy. I have heard rumors that he grew up in Pittsburgh, beat the accent out of himself like a penitent with his scourge. For all I know, he never even attended college, though he seems to have the autodidact's insight into a buffet of topics. Someone once saw him wearing a Notre Dame baseball cap and now the thought is that he was raised Catholic.

He smiles graciously when the waitress approaches the table, and then orders for both of us like I'm his date. "*Pivo, prosím,*" he says and flashes a thumb and forefinger to indicate two. An older Czech couple sitting across the room watch him with the dead fish stares that seem to be some kind of talisman against Americans.

"You'll have to tell me where you found Holly," I say.

He laughs and shakes his head but waves my comment away. "No, no, no," he says. "She found me. But look, I have to talk to you about something important, and confidential. It's about money. Anna is broke."

Stephanie was half right; it was about Anna. But she was wrong about the timing; the first beer has yet to even be poured.

"Broke? I didn't even know there was any trouble."

"Well, you wouldn't."

"No," I say. "But the Globe. There's no danger there, is there?"

Michael shakes his head. "We keep our money separate. For years it was a condition of her family that I not have any direct access to her money. We could always petition for small grants, so to speak—that's how we got the seed money for the Globe—but for the most part, what's mine is mine and what's hers is hers."

"But what happened?"

"The well has run dry," he says. "No, that's not strictly true. Her uncle, who's the head of the family, has made a couple of colossal investment mistakes."

Michael allows me time for this information to sink in, nodding occasionally as if to encourage the thoughts that from his vantage point must be parading across my face.

"Apparently, he had a chance to get in on some natural gas scheme in Russia. So he sold out of what had been a diversified portfolio and rolled a tremendous amount of the family capital into it. In all fairness, it should have worked. If I had known about it, I'd have probably told him to go for it. People have been quietly making money in Russia for years now. Something clearly went wrong. The man in charge of the venture was arrested by the government and all his assets seized—including her uncle's stake."

"Holy shit."

Michael leans back in his chair and delivers me a look, as if to say: *Yes, holy shit indeed.*

"You can imagine," he says, "that to a woman like Anna this is incredibly disturbing. She's forty-five years old and has never truly thought about money in any important way. It's like water in the kitchen faucet. Always she has turned on whatever she needed, hot or cold, and it just came pouring out. Now, nothing."

"Well, it's not like cancer or starvation or—"

"No, it's infinitely worse. It's petulant tantrums and drunken episodes like trying to ruin Stephanie's night by setting you up with a little minx like Holly. She's insufferable, really. Overnight, she's transformed from an interesting, sophisticated woman who can speak four languages to a foot-stomping teenager with the rhetorical strategies of that little girl from *The Exorcist.*"

"Jesus. What are you going to do?"

"I'm going to show her how to make her own money. Don't ask me how just yet—I'm still working that out. What she needs now is a decent chunk to get her started."

"Are you going to give her something from the Globe?"

"I'm not giving that bitch a penny," he says. "Don't worry, she and I are fine. In fact, her sudden poverty has raised her lowly American husband quite high in her esteem. When she hasn't been the most ridiculous person alive, she's actually been quite attentive. No, the marriage is fine."

"Thank God."

This makes Michael laugh, just as the waitress brings over two brimming Pilsner Urquells in their signature glasses. His laughter is timed in such a way that I can tell the waitress thinks he might be laughing at her. She looks from Michael to me and then quickly at the beers in case they are the genesis, somehow, of all this mirth. She is thin and too blonde to be natural, but she's young and so all mistakes can be forgiven. In fact, it's clear that she has the blind, unearned confidence of youth, because her reaction to Michael's laughter is to compose her face into an expression so haughty it is nearly a caricature of the Central European mask. But then, Michael places his hand on her wrist and looks her directly in the eye and says, *"Děkuji,"* with a surprising sincerity. All is forgiven.

When the waitress has taken our order and gone away, Michael says, "My wife is incredibly talented. In a way, this is a great opportunity for her."

"I'm excited to see what she will do."

"Me, too."

We drink for a moment from our beers and I think of what Anna might do with herself. I think of several things that she might find interesting, but none of them will make her any money.

"Where will her initial investment come from?" I say.

"That's where you come in, my friend."

Astonishment is a word in English that does not always live up to the promise of its meaning. Michael will not give his own wife money but expects that I will fund her? *My friend.* You are confusing me with a wealthier man.

"I don't mean that you're to give her money." He laughs at my no doubt absurd expression. "Henry, you must think I'm an asshole."

"No," I say stupidly.

"Yes," he says. "But you're a good man. You probably would have scrounged up more money than you could afford and given it to Anna. And with Stephanie's blessing. And *that* is part of the reason I've told you so much."

"Well . . ."

"Well nothing. You're a romantic, Henry. You love gestures. I've known that ever since you told me how many times you went to see the Depardieu version of *Cyrano de Bergerac* in college."

"Seven times," I say. "I only stopped because the projectionist started hitting on me."

"He should have known you were in love with Roxane."

"He should have."

"Okay," Michael says, "so here's the deal. Anna's uncle feels bad that he's left her in such a state and so he's offered her a little something. Apparently, there was an aunt, dead nearly seven years now, who had been a bibliophile. Anna has fond memories of her, you know, images of her aunt's personality— a graceful woman sitting in an armchair in a big library by the fire, a drink in one hand and some Russian classic in the other. Since Anna had such close feelings for the woman, the uncle has offered her the entire collection. It is several thousand volumes."

I let out a low, appreciative whistle. "Did this aunt have taste?" I ask.

"That's what we want you to find out," Michael says. "We'd like you to go up there—the uncle lives outside Brno—and catalogue the collection, work up an estimate of its value, and create a plan for disposing of the books."

"You want to sell them all?"

Michael shrugs his shoulders. "I'm sure Anna will become sentimental and keep back a few, but yes, the bulk of the collection will have to go."

"Wow."

"You'll get your percentage, of course. This isn't meant to be charity," Michael says. "I just want somebody I can trust doing the work."

"Selling a collection of that size will take some time."

"That's not a problem. As I've told you, we don't even know what we're going to do with the money yet."

"I'm incredibly flattered," I say, "but wouldn't a Czech dealer be more appropriate?"

"Ah, I forgot to mention. Nearly the entire collection is in English. No," Michael says, "you're perfect."

"What's the uncle like?"

"You're going to like him. He's an old rascal."

It is then that the food arrives. Meats in dark gravy, dumplings, heavy bread. We order another round of beer. We do not laugh at the waitress, we pay no particular mind to the old Czech couple across the way. Instead, we simply dig in, filling our bellies with food that has been comforting the ill at ease for generations. And who wouldn't let themselves be comforted?

We arrive at New Town Hall and buy our tickets for the exhibit whose title, loosely translated, is "Prague and Its Long Relationship with the Devil." The New Town Hall is anything but new. Built in the late 14th century, the long meeting hall is shadowed by the tower, whose top floor provides a striking view of the city. The walls on the ground floor are new plaster and shockingly white, and there is an impressive staircase that narrows with each flight the visitor travels. Paintings, part of a separate and longer-running show, are hung sporadically throughout the tower. No one seems to be in charge. Once the tickets are purchased we are on our own. There are no little tags to wear, no hand stamps, no audio recording explaining the works on display, no museum workers in maroon or green or black jackets to help people along. And as far as I can tell, no security whatsoever.

As we walk in and begin to consult the brochure, Michael taps my arm and points into the corner on the first floor where there are two sawhorses, a band saw, and bits of lumber lying around unattended. A lawsuit waiting to happen in Boston or Chicago or San Francisco, but not in Prague. Here the people know that life is dangerous and, for the most part, governments are powerless to protect them from it. Michael smiles at me, two little red patches shining on his cheeks from all the beer we drank with lunch. I can tell that he'd rather skip this altogether and keep drinking now that his real business has been taken care of.

Michael and I ascend the staircase with the too careful pace of drunks, our eyes cast down to secure the placement of feet on each step. Michael keeps a flask of Johnnie Walker in his jacket pocket and I half expect him to stop on each landing and take a long pull. He's already done this once, out on the street in front of the tower, before we bought the tickets. "A man who has lost half his wealth is entitled to drink whenever he sees fit," he'd said.

At a window on one of the landings, I pause to look down on the street below. Surprised, Michael walks over to join me. For a few moments we stand there together in silence.

"Okay," Michael says. "What are we looking at?" He's not annoyed, just befuddled, ready to do what we've come to do and move on.

"You must have heard of the defenestrations."

"Yes."

"One of them occurred here."

"At this window?"

"One of these windows."

Michael leans against the sill and then out over the ledge. There's no glass to stop him, just open air inviting you to jump into the sky. At night there are enormous wooden shutters that are pulled closed and bolted. For a second I think he's drunk enough to fall, but he is not, only playing with me as usual, trying to create something for himself, looking to make the moment somehow remarkable. This is why people love Michael Leo.

He says, "It would be an unpleasant distance to fall."

"Very."

I had never even heard the word defenestration until I'd moved to the Czech Republic. The First Defenestration of

Prague took place right here in the 15th century when angry residents of the Nové Město demanded the release of citizens who had been arrested for having the wrong political sympathies. Eventually, the mob broke in and threw three town councillors and seven of Prague's leading citizens to their deaths. It happened again in the 17th century, as part of ongoing strife between Catholics and Protestants; two of the king's councillors had been seized and thrown from the windows of the chancellery. An event that is often attributed as the genesis of the Thirty Years' War.

Apparently, throwing people out of windows is a thing here, a fitting metaphor for the city's political history. At the very least it is a story to give you pause on a quiet Sunday afternoon as you make your way to see an exhibit of rare books on the subject of the occult.

Finally, we arrive at the third-floor exhibit. There are four glass cases positioned against each wall of the main room. In each case are four books on display. The texts are softly lit from above, and on the wall hang posters describing the work and its author. The books are very old indeed, the most recent dating to 1844. Each one is a little miracle, despite its subject matter, to have survived the centuries intact and in generally good repair.

I am a little bit in awe, as I always am when I come face to face with an old book. Partly, I have a highly developed sense of nostalgia, but also I can't help but think of this object's history, the hands that made it, the people who have turned the pages, licking a forefinger occasionally as they went. Especially these books: the *Dictionnaire Infernal, Formicarius,* and, of course, the book that has drawn me here.

I look to see Michael's reaction to the displays. He raises an eyebrow. "There it is," I say. "Do you see the poster?"

There are two posters, in fact, for this book—one a facsimile of the title page, the other an enlargement of one of the engravings. It is impossible not to look: a line drawing of a naked woman lying on her back, trussed up in such a way that her wrists are bound to her ankles, her large breasts flopping obscenely on either side of her chest.

"That's an interesting choice," Michael says of the enlarged engraving.

"Compared to some, that's tame."

The Malleus Maleficarum, or *The Hammer of the Witches.* First published in 1487 by Heinrich Kramer and Jacob Sprenger. This is the Cologne edition of 1520. It is a book that I've read in translation, in paperback, a book that has been the central feature of multiple films and lent its name to others, a text that educated our ancestors in the art of hunting witches. I look at this particular book and cannot help but think about the hands of the Inquisitor.

Beside us is an elderly couple. The man is thin and frail-looking with steel-gray hair in a long sheet to his shoulders. The lenses of his eyeglasses are so thick I imagine him being able to read billboard advertisements on Saturn. His wife is diminutive, her hair a puffy white cloud like a bichon frise. Both wear light blue cardigan sweaters, even in the summer heat. They are speaking Spanish. They look at the book, open to the page with the engraving, then up to the poster, then back to the book. They seem mystified. I wonder if they came to see the exhibit on purpose or if they just happened upon it by accident.

"How much is it worth?" Michael asks.

"Why?" I say. "Do you want to steal it?"

"Don't think it hasn't crossed my mind."

We stare for a minute at the thick boards that can be secured together with metal clasps, the heavy paper of the pages, the ink that looks just as fresh now as it must have five hundred years ago.

"The book is in three sections," I tell Michael. "The first tries to establish that witchcraft is a real phenomenon. It argues that the devil exists, that he is powerful and can do great works, and so it's natural that he should have people on Earth to help him. The second section discusses how to identify a witch. Often, it says, the devil will create some hardship in the life of an otherwise good woman that will plant the seed of doubt in her faith and make her susceptible to pacts that promise to solve her troubles. Or, the devil will expose young women to handsome creatures and ensnare them that way. The third part instructs the would-be inquisitor how to set up a court, how to deal with local opposition and, most importantly"—I point up at the engraving of the bound female figure—"how to interrogate witches so as to be able to get the best kinds of confessions. They tortured the women naked so that no witchcraft could be concealed in their clothing."

"Sounds like they were covering every angle."

The woman looks at her husband and then shakes a finger at

the book. "*Diabolico,*" she says. "*Tck, tck, tck, tck.*" He nods at her seriously, no doubt fearing to contradict her. I know I would be afraid. I have visions of her confessing this visit to her priest and performing half a dozen additional Hail Marys.

Michael puts his face very close to the glass in order to get a better look at the original engraving. "I wonder what these artists thought," he says. "That they were doing God's work? Looks more like pornography."

The old lady may or may not know English, but it's clear that she recognized that last word. She turns to Michael, looking slightly aghast, and I think it takes every ounce of self-control she has not to *tck, tck, tck, tck* him too. I am in some ways enchanted with this woman. She is a dying breed, perhaps. I cannot imagine either Anna or Stephanie in her old age looking at five-hundred-year-old engravings in a rare book and mustering any kind of outrage. Perhaps soon we will be beyond outrage. One world passeth away, I think, while another stumbles in. A world devoid of righteous old ladies.

Maybe, I think suddenly, I will ask Selma when she arrives if there will still be righteous old ladies in the Muslim world. I will tell her the story of our visit here to this exhibit, describe for her the *Malleus Maleficarum* and our little old Spanish lady's reaction. Probably she will think I am mad, or at least ridiculous. She will think my mind is occupied with bizarre things, and she will quietly ask Stephanie to cancel any plans I may have had of introducing her to literary Prague. And maybe she will be right to do it.

"From our perspective," Michael says, "the politics of this

book seem screamingly obvious. It's a play to consolidate power, maybe even a desperate one. Solidify the church's patriarchal hold on society by demonizing women. It's kinky, but kind of pathetic."

Michael is sobering. The drunken buoyancy that delivered him up all those flights of steps is wearing off. He doesn't want to be here with me, has no particular interest in this book or maybe any other that wasn't written in, say, the last seventy-five years. Even this estimate might be generous. But since he is here, and on the receiving end of dirty looks from elderly Spanish ladies, he might as well make a good show of it. He is standing over this old and controversial text and delivering his coffeehouse arguments.

I look down at the book and then back up at the poster. "I think you've watched *The Da Vinci Code* one too many times," I say.

The Spanish couple begin the long, slow walk down the staircase, out of this room and into what's left of their lives. The book for them is left behind. We stare down at it together, our elbows resting on the glass. "I wish we could touch it," Michael says. "I'd like to turn the pages and look at the other engravings."

But of course that's impossible. I look for a moment at the expression on his face. It is concentrated and a little desperate, and that's when it hits me. Michael has not told me the whole truth about Anna's money troubles. Their finances, perhaps, are not so separate as he would have me believe. The Globe is in danger and, maybe, so is their marriage. Stephanie, had she

been here, would have known right away. I am not just doing
them a favor by looking at the dead aunt's collection. I may
be keeping them solvent, among other things. That's why he
doesn't want to discuss Anna's plans for the money. She doesn't
have any and never will.

I clap my hand gently on Michael's back. I can feel the heat
of his body even through the fabric of his blazer. He seems
surprised when I touch him, startled, as though I've brought
him back from some deep analysis of the engraving. I, however,
think I know better. Michael's mind is certainly someplace, but
not in the 15th or 16th century, and certainly not preoccupied
by witchcraft or Inquisitions. I rub my hand on his back again
in a way that I hope is comforting.

"Come on," I say. "Let's get out of here, too."

———

It's nearly five o'clock when Michael drops me off. We had
spent longer at lunch than I'd originally thought. The apartment has a Sunday quietude and a warm smell to it, the oil in the
hardwood floors having baked in the sun for hours and hours,
a vase with daisies that are past their prime. I want to feel good
and believe that the weekend has been successful: Stephanie's
party, the ritual of our Sunday morning coffee, the rare books
exhibit at the New Town Hall—not forgetting my late-night
pilgrimage to the river. But something is stopping me. Part of
it is that I'm sobering up myself now, my mouth dry and thick.
What I want is a big glass of water and some time with my

wife to explain all that I've learned today and all that I suspect. There are days, I realize, that I rely on her to help me process the world. Maybe we'll cook something simple together, drink half a bottle of Beaujolais, play a game of Scrabble. Or even better, I think, lie on the couch, our feet by each other's elbows, and read our books quietly—alone together.

For a moment, I stand in front of the refrigerator, drinking the water and letting the cool air drift over me. In the background I can hear a car or two passing on the street outside and, behind that, another noise. It is low and rhythmic and disturbingly familiar—a sound that lives right on the edge of consciousness but won't quite let itself get pinned down. When the traffic noise subsides, I can hear it more clearly. I follow the sound down the hall and into the bedroom.

When I open the door, there is Stephanie. She is sitting up in bed, her back resting sturdily against the headboard. And lying there with her, her dark head in Stephanie's lap, is Selma. She is sobbing, the sounds the unguarded sorrow of childhood before we know about decorum or self-possession or any of that. Just pure emotion.

"No, no, no-oo," she seems to be saying, "No, no, no-oo." Over and over again. It is heartbreaking to listen to, and I can see Stephanie's eyes are wet with her own tears, even as she strokes her friend's hair and makes murmuring sounds of comfort.

"Hello, Henry," Stephanie eventually says.

Selma immediately sits up and her wailing stops. She looks at me once, a look of such complexity—sorrow, horror, mortification—all wrapped together as one. Mascara is running down from her eyes and her skin is blotchy and irritated.

"Oh my God," she says, sniffing. "Henry."

"It's me," I say stupidly. And then, "I'll leave you two alone."

I don't even exchange a look with Stephanie. I just back out and shut the door behind me. I stand there for several seconds with my hand on the doorknob almost unable to move. Selma will be ashamed. She might even decide to leave. Was she due to arrive today? Quickly, I try to think back over everything I'm supposed to know about Selma's visit (remarkably little) and realize I can't think of anything.

Good lord, what's happening now?

Three

Stephanie's friends are, well, *spooky* is the word I've always used. To say that they were all more than friends would be like shyly admitting that Czechs do, indeed, seem to have a fondness for beer. Even after a decade of marriage, I have not been able to shake the strange combination of fascination and fear that strikes me whenever one or, God forbid, all of the women are present. My unease, let's call it, stems from something that is like a vibration felt in the too quiet air or a stray scent that troubles you in its elusiveness. My wife's friends have many of the common attributes of longtime female compatriots: They finish each other's sentences, have bizarrely unfunny inside jokes that more often than not lead to the singing of show tunes from *Grease* or *The Sound of Music*, they steal and re-steal each other's clothing, have jealousies over bigger eyes, bigger boobs, smaller butts, have even more bitter rivalries over men shared, discarded, and lost. More than any of these things, however, they are viciously protective of each other's lives and happiness. And Selma is their prize, the best among them, to be loved and coveted, and perhaps even worshipped, until the gloss of her soul has become so high as to shine brightly against any darkness.

Still, Selma was a late arrival to their little group. It all began in northern Virginia—just, just outside the District—in a neighborhood that no one under the age of forty should have been able to rent in, let alone buy property, on a street called Coventry Drive. The house they shared together was enormous, a gabled and turreted six-bedroom with a brand-new tin roof that had to have been some young architect's dream. Two Filipino sisters owned the house, Charlotte and Clementine. Or rather, their wealthy father did, a successful real estate broker, who decided that it made more sense to buy a house for his daughters while they slugged their way through graduate programs than to burn money on rent. So, there was Charlotte, a future radiologist, and Clementine (Clem, Clemmy, Clemin-pop, Clembo-kin, depending on their moods), a future professor of Women's Studies via sociology. And then came, one by one, our carefully vetted clan of renters: Margaret, Audrey, and Stephanie. Margaret was blonde and tall and graceful, spoke three languages, and loved her work in an Oregon senator's office. She was voted most likely to marry some ambitious schmuck, rise spectacularly, and then fall just as spectacularly, in the vein of Jackie Kennedy Onassis. Audrey was shorter and curvier, a nurse with a particular fetish for black doctors (the combination is apparently irresistible) about whom she loved to tell racy stories while downing bottomless glasses of pinot grigio. And finally, Stephanie, who would eventually become *my* Stephanie. Daughter of a famous political father, rail thin then like the youngest, shyest schoolgirl, the athlete of the group, a runner whose ribbons and medals decorated the top of a dresser in her immaculate third-floor bedroom, who said she would never marry — didn't see the point in it — and who, for the longest time, was the group's mascot and always pulled into the center of every photograph, strands of her long hair inevitably clinging to someone's lip gloss as they leaned in to squish her.

They were perfectly happy, the five of them. Lived like that together for three years. But just as Charlotte began her residency and Clem her dissertation, just when Margaret was considering the proposal of a young Republican lawyer from North Carolina, and Audrey hooked up with the Wesley Snipes of her dreams, and Stephanie was dreading daily the Foreign Service examination, Selma came to take her place in that sixth (and last) bedroom.

It was Clem who had brought her home one night for dinner. It had been Margaret's turn to cook and Stephanie's to buy the wine. All six of them seem to remember the night perfectly. The meal had been a pasta primavera, fresh bread, and a chocolate cake for dessert. At the end of three hours, drunk and rosy-cheeked, Audrey said, "It's obvious, Selma has to come and live with us." And it was, apparently, obvious to them all. Though if you ask why, if you ask what, exactly, it was about Selma's personality that had attracted them and compelled such an invitation, none of them could really say. Only that they loved her and knew it. The one time I pushed Stephanie on the subject she said, "Some things just don't need to be *explained*." Eventually, however, I would come to understand.

I will never forget the first time I met them all. Stephanie and I had been introduced at a Red Cross benefit for rape victims in the former Yugoslavia. I had been selling books from a table that had been set up by Politics and Prose Bookstore, a hefty portion of the proceeds going that night to the charity. Eventually, I found the courage to ask her out for coffee. Three weeks later, as things progressed, she said, "I can't keep seeing you if I don't bring you home for dinner." Of course, I'd heard all about the house on Coventry Drive and its residents. I was intimidated. Here I was, a minimum-wage bookseller with what felt like a two-bit bachelor's degree, being brought before a group of educated and sophisticated women to be judged. I couldn't imagine a way to win them over. Not women this tight-knit. Stephanie had warned that they were all so close that their menstrual cycles had become synchronized. At that time I had never even heard of such a phenomenon and couldn't, *couldn't*, get the detail out of my head.

"So," I said as we pulled into the drive in front of their house, "what you're telling me is that all six of you have your period right now, together."

"As it turns out," she said and grinned a little crazily. Then seeing my discomfort, she added, "Don't worry, I'll take care of you."

Of course I was charmed if not any less intimidated. Her hair then was so long and shining and beautiful, and when she smiled her whole face lit up with delight in a way I'd never seen before. Stephanie could have been leading me to the slaughter — I could even have known it — and nothing would have made the slightest bit of difference.

That's what it is, I suppose, to be a man.

We weren't even out of the car when Audrey swung open the front door and skipped out to greet us, all friendly, happy smiles, just a little drunk already, exuding a kind of warmth and familiarity that I'd rarely ever seen among even close friends. Perhaps, I have always thought, it was a tactical move to send out Audrey first. Though at the time I just basked in a momentary sense of relief.

I barely had time to take in the exterior of the house before I was ushered inside. Stephanie had not prepared me for how they lived. This was no graduate student collective with clean but mismatched furniture. This house should have been in a magazine. This house had been decorated: Philippe Starck chairs, Tom Dixon lighting. It had a purpose. I was so stupid then I didn't even know how impressed I should have been. All I knew was that everything seemed to glitter and resonate, texture against texture, to create a truly stunning effect. I couldn't imagine how any of them ever managed to leave the house. But in my twenties, I didn't yet know it was possible to get used to anything.

"Whoa," I blurted out.

"Nice, huh?" Audrey said.

"That's an understatement."

Reaching for her wineglass where she'd left it on a little table in the entryway, Audrey gave me a look that should have been my first warning, a look that said *Of course it is, honey.*

By the end of the night, I was in love with all of them. They had a family room that had been turned into a library—the literary collections of all six women that I was permitted to browse through, drink in hand, while they all talked incessantly around me. Charlotte had cooked a brisket with asparagus and new potatoes and said, "We thought a man would want red meat," and laughed crazily like it was the greatest joke. Though we finished the meal by eating chocolate mousse out of espresso cups with dainty silver spoons. There was the "family" dog, a Dalmatian mix named Miss Lemon, who rested her head in your lap while you ate and looked up at you with soulful, wishful eyes, waiting patiently for you to drop her a morsel. She actually belonged to Margaret, the only dog lover in the bunch. All the rest of them had exactly one cat each, all toms, to whom I was introduced during the course of the evening: Cheerio, of course, and Juniper, Maximilian, Crackers, and Squirt. After dinner a fire was lit in the family room, the fireplace tall enough to have roasted an entire pig on a spit, the edges blackened with use. We played Scrabble in teams and drank dry sherry, but I mostly watched them laughing and talking, their hands in constant motion, their voices alternately smooth and raucous, the pitch seeming to rise and fall like an incantation.

And, of course, there was Selma.

She wasted no time in making an impression on me. Sometime after one, the fire was allowed to burn itself out and the friends began to say goodnight to each other and take dirty dishes to the kitchen for washing in the morning. For a moment, I found myself alone with Selma. She had been very welcoming all night and I told her what a wonderful time I'd had and thanked her. She nodded and gave me a weak smile; it was obvious something was on her mind. "You seem like a nice enough boy," she said quietly. I said I hoped so. "But if you hurt Stephanie," she said, "we'll make you regret it."

Later, drunk beneath the covers of Stephanie's bed, I said, "You guys are scary as hell."

"Who's scary?"

"All of you: Charlotte, Clementine, Margaret, Audrey, *Selma* (I found I couldn't say her name without somehow exaggerating it)—even you."

"Even me?"

"Even you. But you're all so lovely too. It's overwhelming."

"We're just women."

"Well, maybe that's your mistake."

"We're not women?"

"Not *just* women."

There were things I would need to explain to Stephanie. In the town where I grew up people didn't write dissertations or have libraries (except the public one) or eat chocolate mousse from espresso cups or drink dry sherry while they played Scrabble. Instead, we ate our meat loaf and mashed potatoes at 5 PM, did the dishes directly after, and settled in with the television. Sometimes my grandmother read a paperback romance, but mostly there would be small talk between commercial breaks about the best way to remove a stain on the living room carpet—and these conversations might go on for as long as thirty minutes. I knew more about cleaning products, the restorative powers of lemon juice and toothpaste, and even the very techniques for scrubbing than I did almost anything else. I had not resented my childhood, but even then, and as often as not through the pages of books I checked out from that public library, I realized that there were indeed larger ways to live. Even if the expanse, the breadth, the depth were nowhere except in your own mind. I didn't, in any practical way, know how someone like me would achieve this new way of living. Especially not the scrawny, moody, generally withdrawn adolescent that I had been; at thirteen, already working on the loading dock of the local plant nursery throwing fifty-pound bags of mulch into the backs of people's station wagons. I guessed that money was involved and so saved nearly every penny I made. But I somehow also sensed that something like money wouldn't be enough, and I would have to learn what to do with money if I was ever so lucky as to get enough of it. No, what I learned from reading so many novels was that people were the real agent of change in the lives of others. And particularly relationships between men and women. *Women.* But not just any women.

It was a revelation of this kind that came into focus for me that first night on Coventry Drive and no doubt later made me appreciate the relationships that men like Michael Leo had with women like Anna Nemcova.

"I wish you could switch places with me," Stephanie said, her lips brushing my temple, "just for a day. Then you could see that we're not really so mysterious."

"No, that's all right. This close is just close enough." I squeezed her tightly and she giggled. "Besides, mystery is exciting."

"You're thinking of Selma now, aren't you?" she said. "I saw the way you were looking at her after dinner."

"I was looking at all of you. It's like a minefield when you're all in the same room."

"We are pretty hot." Stephanie sat up in bed then for a moment and piled her hair on top of her head and tied it there. All except for one wispy lock that graced the back of her suddenly exposed neck.

"I had a little bit of a run-in with Selma."

"What kind?"

"She told me not to hurt you or she—*they*—will make me regret it."

"Oh God, I'm sorry," Stephanie said, clamping a hand over her mouth. "But she wasn't kidding. So you'll just have to be careful with me."

"I never intended to do anything else."

For several minutes we kissed and touched and smelled each other. Did I know then that this woman would be my wife? Perhaps not just yet.

"Still, Selma doesn't seem to like me."

"Oh she likes you fine," Stephanie said. "But it's a little bit complicated."

"What does that mean?"

"That means that we seem to have this unspoken policy as a group to distrust all men but individually, almost secretly, be obsessed with the ones in our lives."

"Bizarre."

"Not really. And besides, it's working out well for you."

Stephanie lay back against me with her head on my shoulder, trying to learn how to mold herself into the angles and contours of my body. For a while she kept squirming around, making little adjustments, until she found a place she liked, with both of us staring at the room's high ceiling. She had the stereo cycling Dave Matthews Band's "Crash into Me" over and over again. In the light of the stereo, I could see much of the shadowed room: the running trophies, the framed photographs of her father, who had been two Republican presidents' ambassador to Argentina, a pile of dirty clothes lying on the floor of the open closet door (giving me, perhaps, a first indication of my future domestic life), a framed poster of Paris at night and another of the cover of James Joyce's *Ulysses*, which went a long way toward further charming me. At first I thought that moonlight was spilling through the room as well, but when I mentioned it Stephanie just laughed and said that was romantic, but really it was only a streetlight.

However, on the sill of that window from which the light shone, there was a collection of stones arranged in descending order of size from left to right. And I felt, oddly, that I could love a woman who collected rocks, who read books, who had ambitions—on her desk was the dictionary-size tome that she was using to help prepare her for the Foreign Service exam—who had wonderfully complex and interesting friends. I could love a woman who knew how to buy wine, who could make important distinctions about the sexual politics of men and women. It seemed, though it was only later that I would think of it in this way, that a wonderful spell had been cast upon me—one that knew me and my needs intimately, that somehow saw into the holes in my young life and promised, sweetly, to fill them.

It was perfect, this young woman lying next to me, talking in the dark; she was completely oblivious to the transformation that was taking place beside her. She spoke, exhaling some small thing from her life on Coventry Drive, and I inhaled it and let it infect me. Was it a poison? A cancer? A curse? Or maybe a protection against all these things?

"You know about Audrey, right?" she said. "That she likes black men?"

"Yes."

"She seems to want to tell anybody who will listen."

"Well, about a year ago she was dating this absolutely gorgeous doctor named Roy. We all liked him. He was scary charming. I mean, really, the man didn't seem able to strike a false note."

"You gotta hate people like that."

"And of course Audrey was absolutely smitten. She came home with stories of their sexual exploits and all the crazy things he was getting her to do."

"Crazy in a bad way?"

"Well, I wouldn't have done them. But Audrey seemed totally into it, so who am I to judge?"

"I bet you secretly wanted to do those crazy things too."

"Funny you should say that."

"Uh, oh. Why do I have a feeling I'm not going to like this?"

"One afternoon I came home from campus and no one was in sight, which was unusual. With six of us, there's nearly always somebody home. *And* I saw Roy's Lexus parked on the street. So I figured he was here with Audrey."

"Right."

"Right," she said. But she gave this look. "As soon as I walked in I could hear them, you know, doing it. I didn't care. I thought it was kind of great. I mean, the bed was thumping and she was screaming. We've got kind of used to listening to each other."

"That's going to make me self-conscious now," I said.

"Try not to worry. Anyway, I'd been hearing for weeks how awesome the sex was with Roy and so I got a little curious."

"You went and spied on them?"

"Maybe."

"Damn, you're bad."

"Wait. There's more. As I was sneaking up the stairs, the noises became clearer and clearer. I mean, they were really going at it, and I thought, *Shit*. You know? But as I got to the hallway outside Audrey's room I realized that's not where they were."

"Where were they? Not this room?"

"No. They were in Charlotte's room. So I snuck over to Charlotte's door and peeked in."

"And you saw Roy and Charlotte."

"You got it."

"Wow."

"Wow is right. I'd never seen anybody else have sex in my life. I mean, he was taking her from behind and Charlotte was loving it. I hardly recognized her. She was someplace else entirely."

"Did it turn you on?"

"No, I was horrified. Now I had this information that I didn't want to have."

"Did you tell?"

"No. In the end, I didn't have to. But the whole thing came out into the open and it was ugly."

"Maybe this is a stupid question, but why did Charlotte do it?"

"Turned out that Roy had a thing for Asian girls."

"Huh," I almost snorted. "That's funny, but it doesn't really answer my question."

"No, it doesn't."

For a minute or two we lay there quietly and I could tell that Stephanie had managed to unsettle herself a little. I held her tighter and kissed that place at the end of her jawline and under her ear that would become our favorite. That got me a smile.

"I guess Audrey was upset," I said.

"To say the least. Maybe you can tell that Audrey has a little problem with drinking? It's not too bad, not intervention bad or anything, but she's always thought of herself as the inelegant ugly duckling of the group—though God knows we've tried and tried to convince her otherwise."

"Her beauty is different from everyone else's."

"Yes, and when Roy went for Charlotte she just became unhinged. She drank a bottle of wine every night, said all kinds of ugly things about everybody, not just Charlotte. Actually, it came out that I knew and didn't tell and so she was righteously pissed at me, too."

"I'm surprised you all got over something like that."

"Sometimes so am I. It was Selma who hit upon what to do."

Stephanie paused for a moment, like she was gathering herself. I didn't say anything, just let her find her own way.

"One Sunday afternoon the six of us found ourselves together in the family room. It had been the first time we'd all been together since Roy and Charlotte got caught. Audrey was playing the silence card and Charlotte was looking ashamed of herself, but also searching for a way to own what she'd done as well. Selma sat quietly on her end of one of the couches with fancy colored paper and a pair of scissors. I didn't know what she was doing. I thought maybe she was doing some kind of weird Arab origami or something. Clem and Margaret had just decided to try to mediate between Charlotte and Audrey, saying all the usual things about how men sucked and that their friendship was bigger and more important than anything else."

"How did that work?"

"How do you think? It was all absolutely true, of course, but that didn't make a bit of difference to Audrey. In fact, their attempts at reconciliation only got them fighting. Charlotte and Audrey were actually standing face to face and screaming at each other when Selma stood up and unfurled a sheet of exactly half a dozen paper dolls.

"It was such a crazily unexpected move that for a moment we all just stared at her and watched as Selma snipped each doll from the hands of the others and then picked up a black marker from the coffee table and in big, block letters wrote ROY across the head of the doll. Then she held the little paper doll by its hands so that everyone could see, kissed it on the forehead, and then turned and threw it into the fireplace, where it curled and disintegrated in seconds."

"Shit."

"Then Selma looked at me, then at the dolls, then back to me, and I knew what she wanted us to do. So I stood up and wrote Roy's name on the doll and threw it in the fire. We all did it, one by one, and Charlotte and Audrey burned theirs last."

"Did it work?"

"Well, if you mean did we all put Roy behind us and remain friends, I would guess the answer is self-evident."

"Why did you tell me that story?" I said.

"You seemed to want to understand what Selma said to you."

"Great, now I feel even worse," I said. "In fact, where did you put my clothes?" But I was mostly joking and Stephanie knew it, too. Still, she clung to me tightly.

"You're not going anywhere, boy."

"No?"

"No."

The rest, as they say, is history. I never did manage to get away, and as I had hoped it would, my marriage to Stephanie changed my life utterly. Now, here I am a decade later in the living room of our apartment in Prague trying to entertain Selma (she *had* arrived early) while Stephanie goes out to find something to cook for dinner—not an easy task at this hour on a Sunday. I sit in a leather club chair across from the couch where Selma has arranged herself with legs curled underneath her. She looks like a wounded animal trying to make itself as small as possible. Not the woman who had me quaking on Coventry Drive, a woman whose charisma I'd found frankly overwhelming. Now there is just this small person for whom I feel only a surprising tenderness.

"How's Mansour?" I ask quietly.

"Much as you might expect. Depressed mostly. Bitter." Even after so long in the United States, Selma still has that tinge of an accent.

Now that Selma's sitting up and speaking, it's possible to really look at her. The only signs of age I can see in her are the lightest of laugh lines around her mouth. Faint, faint. Almost nothing. Her hair, though looking a little rumpled, is still soft and bright with life, her skin taut, her figure inviting. I try very hard to stay focused on Mansour.

"Of course he's bitter," I say. "If I were him, I'd be a hell of a lot more than bitter."

"He was at first. I'm sure he'd be glad to know you're angry on his behalf." There, that little moment. *I'm sure he'd be glad to know you're angry on his behalf.* A certain ironic, negligent superiority, straight from Coventry Drive. How do they do it? What do they know about the world that I do not?

Selma must have some news about her husband, though. There's been a serious legal effort.

"His lawyers must have something to report after all this time," I say.

"You'd be surprised by how little."

"Can they just hold him like this, indefinitely, without charging him with something?"

Selma smiles.

"They can," she says. "Everyone was surprised at first. It's America, right? But Mansour is not a citizen, he's living on a visa that can be revoked just as easily as it was given. The lawyers say that if he hasn't done anything he'll have to eventually be released."

"How long has it been?"

"Fourteen months."

I raise my eyebrows and shake my head. I try to imagine what it would be like to have a year of my life taken away for the mere suspicion that I'd done something wrong.

"As you can see, I'm starting to fall apart a little bit."

"Anybody would," I say. That was good. That was sympathy, genuine and heartfelt. Let's hope she felt it.

"Walking up to your apartment I saw the Kafka statue and laughed. I was just walking along and it bubbled out of me like a snort, like I'd coughed up something. I knew I'd have to talk with you both about what's been happening, and it's just so fucked up I didn't know how to do it. But then I saw that statue and knew: Kafkaesque. That's the only word to describe Mansour's experience and mine. Just close your eyes and imagine men in gray suits and prisoners tied to chairs with roll after roll of red tape."

"Well, if you wanted to come to a place to get perspective on things like that, Prague is absolutely the place."

"*Ya allah*, I know," she said. "I know!"

I wait a moment for Selma to continue, but she seems really to have meant it—everything I need to know about their lives can be explained in one half-baked Kafka reference. Doubtful. There is a package of peppermints on the end table beside me and I carefully peel back the wrapper so that one is exposed, then offer it to Selma. She takes it and smiles and I watch it disappear into her mouth, the white circle lingering for a moment on a flash of pink tongue. I take one myself and then carefully fold the wrapper around the remaining mints. The whole gesture takes perhaps thirty seconds.

Selma seems to be looking beyond me to the buildings across the street as evening falls and lights begin to turn on. I stand up and turn on a few of our own, then stand by one of the windows and look out myself. Something in me suddenly lets go. I absolve myself of all responsibility of managing Selma Al-Khateeb's moment-to-moment happiness and just say the first thing that comes to my mind.

"Prague, I find, can be a comfort."

And that seems, for once, to have been the right thing to say. Selma smiles and jumps up to join me at the window.

"God, I hope so," she says. "You can't imagine how much I've been looking forward to it. There are so many things I want to do here. Though I know I won't amount to anything but a tourist."

There's something about this comment that makes me like Selma, at last. That small insecurity, that she should be something so tasteless, so foolish as a mere tourist snapping pictures and rifling through brochures as she walks through Wenceslas Square. Here was someone you could actually know and like.

"There's nothing wrong with being a tourist," I say.

"Well, I'm a little worried, you know."

"About what?"

"That everyone will think I'm a total shit, visiting the castle and eating out while my husband rots in jail. To come here to be comforted by my friends"—she reaches up to put a hand on my shoulder—"that would be one thing. But to be a tourist, to have *fun*, that would be something else."

My God, I think, do people really talk like this? She's a tragic heroine; I just haven't placed the book yet.

"Well," I say, "be comforted, and if you manage to have a little fun too, we won't tell anyone." And then I open my arms to embrace her. She hesitates for just a moment, then smiles, and I take her in. She is warm, wearing a light cardigan over her T-shirt, and as I hug her to me I feel the softness of her breasts against my chest and the surprising lightness and fragility of her bones. Her scent is not my wife's.

We pull away from each other and smile. "You know, it's almost surreal to be standing here with you in Prague. Every few moments, I think, what the fuck are you doing here, Selma?"

"Well, since you are here," I say, "what do you want to do?"
Selma looks at me, hovering somewhere between concern
and relief. "Honestly? I have no idea. All I want is to do something small and useful—and that doesn't involve governments
and the law."

"Stephanie says you want to see literary Prague."

Selma puts her hand up to her mouth and blushes, just a
little. "God, that sounds so pretentious."

It's only pretentious, I think, if you're pretending. Are you,
Selma Al-Khateeb? And I think quickly about all the energy
it's going to take trying to find out.

"There are a lot of things you might do," I say.

"I wish I hadn't missed Stephanie's party. There was a poetry
reading, wasn't there? And it's embarrassing, but I do want to
see the house Kafka grew up in."

"Well, there's no harm in visiting there."

"I know. But I guess I am interested in actually *doing* something though."

"What were you thinking?"

"Don't laugh."

"I won't. I promise."

"I'd love, love, love to spend some time with you at your
bookstore," she says. "It feels very romantic to me—and far
away from New Jersey prisons."

"That would be easy to arrange."

"You and Stephanie are such a blessing, Henry. Thank you
so much." You're welcome so much. For a moment I zone out,
and Selma can tell. "Are you all right, Henry?"

"Yes, absolutely. Just thinking. Do you still love Madonna? You know, 'Strike a Pose' and all that?"

"Ugh, you remember that?"

"Of course."

"God, forget it the first chance you get."

This gets us laughing, though I had hoped she'd actually do the old routine and vogue for me, but she does not. Still, laughing is how Stephanie finds us when she sweeps into the room, grocery bags full of sausages and potatoes and bread. She also has a bottle of slivovitz. She is smiling when she sees us, but there's a little question there, too, one I know she'll ask me later. I am relieved at the way the room changes when she comes in, and I, like an actor who's just played a small but significant role, can now retire to the wings and watch the stars play out the rest of the drama.

They embrace again, as though they hadn't already seen each other, and then before I know it Stephanie has broken out glasses and is pouring the slivovitz. There are toasts to Selma's arrival, to Mansour's future freedom, to friendship, to life and its mysteries. Before I know it, we have a pretty good little buzz going.

"Wouldn't it be wonderful if everyone could be here?" Stephanie says.

"Hmm. I'm not sure Henry would like that."

"I don't remember asking Henry."

I smile a little bitterly and she sticks her tongue out at me.

"No, really," Stephanie insists, "that's really what you need."

"Maybe," Selma says. "But being here with you is wonderful."

Selma sits on the couch beside Stephanie, so close together that their thighs are touching. She has her arms around Selma and every so often will lean in and rest her head against her friend's. Selma looks pensive, like she can't quite get comfortable, and she's slowly twirling the empty glass in her hand so that the little coating of slivovitz that's left makes patterns against the sides. But even hurt as she is, saddened and rumpled from grief and travel, she still has *it*; she still has that grace that makes every eye find its way to her. In her sadness she looks almost holy. Put a blue cloth on her hair and replace the glass in her hand with an infant and we'd have a perfect Mary.

I have zoned out again. It's Stephanie who notices.

"Didn't we have a great time when Margaret came to visit last year?"

"You did. I had to entertain Jeb. That was two weeks' worth of listening to North Carolina state politics."

"God, I remember now."

Margaret's husband, Jeb, is a state representative who is contemplating making his move to national politics. They live in a big, pillared colonial and Margaret has taken on the role of politician's wife with a little too much ease for Stephanie and the rest of her friends.

"So the first part of the prophesy has come true," Selma says.

"Seems like," Stephanie says. "She's a little Jackie O. Now we just wait for the indiscretion or the tragedy."

"Or both."

And off they go into Coventry Drive gossip. This is Stephanie's role to play in Selma's quest for normalcy. And I know when I'm not needed. In fact, I decide that this is the moment when I should excuse myself and leave them to it. But I don't go far, just to the kitchen, where I start to cook us dinner. The kitchen is open to the living room, and so even peeling potatoes I can see them and, if I want to, follow their conversation.

I have always wondered about the way that Selma fits into their group. There was no secret wish that she suddenly be more like the rest of them. If anything, all the friends have gone a bit too far the other way. And that's perhaps enough to fuck you up. Selma does strike me as remarkable and different. But at what price? It's possible, I think, to smother a person with too much admiration.

Stephanie says, "Did I tell you they own *two* black SUVs? Exactly the same model. I asked her if her house was really the FBI headquarters."

Selma raises her chin a littler higher and smiles. If the FBI reference hurt, it was brief and quickly pushed away.

"Margaret's probably just doing what she thinks she needs to for her husband's career," Selma says.

Stephanie smacks her palm against her forehead. "God, did you hear how that sounds?"

Selma's smile fades a little and she shakes her head, loosening the long hair on one side so that it slides down like a curtain in front of her face. I stop peeling for a moment to watch more closely. I've never seen a woman make that move with another woman before. Hiding behind your hair.

Maybe just a little intervention: "Sounds like a lucky guy to have such a supportive wife."

"What is this, 1950? Let her *support* her husband by living an interesting life," Stephanie says.

Oh my. Apparently she'd been saving this about Margaret for Selma's arrival. How long had she been holding it in?

"Agreed," I say. "And I find Jeb and American politics to be boring as hell, but not everybody has the opportunity to be a U.S. Congressman. It's clearly engrossing. A whole family effort."

"Oh, fuck that," Stephanie says.

"Well," I say, "that is certainly one way to think about it."

Stephanie looks at me and I know she's pissed, but there's something else, too—a grudging admission that she's being unreasonable. She had wanted Selma to be righteous with her and, oddly, it didn't work out that way. I'll probably be in trouble later.

Selma, I find, has been looking at me. Perhaps it doesn't help that I've been standing here arguing with a kitchen knife in my hand. *What have you been feeding this angry woman,* her look seems to say. I want to remind her that tonight's dinner not withstanding, the women around here nourish themselves.

"I just hate to see so much talent go to waste," Stephanie eventually says, trying very hard (I can tell) to keep the edginess out of her voice. "It's just the kind of thing we promised each other we'd never do."

"People make a lot of promises to themselves," I say. "Eventually, we wind up where we're most comfortable."

"Nice," she says derisively.

"Often it is nice."

"I think Margaret was going for a little bit more than nice."

"Sometimes we find ourselves doing things we'd never imagined," Selma says. Stephanie and I just look at Selma. Then I pour myself another shot of slivovitz and knock it back. I've never really liked the stuff. Stephanie knows that, too. Probably she wanted to give Selma the authentic Czech experience.

"I'm sure you're right," I say, and in my head, I can already hear the fight about being passive-aggressive we'll have later. At least I got birthday sex last night.

"So, Henry's going to take you to see where Kafka lived?" Stephanie says.

Selma gathers her hair together into a ponytail and then lets it fall again, perfectly placed around her shoulders. She smiles. "Yes, Kafka's house and to his bookstore."

What's on her face that surprises me, though, is this: I'm here to escape my life, my jailed husband, my general lack of direction, but also now, Stephanie, I'm here to escape you.

———◦◦◦———

Dinner is delicious, even if I do say so myself. The potatoes are especially appreciated, pan-fried with onions and sprinkled with fresh paprika we bought on a recent trip to Budapest. Selma is shown into the study where the couch has a pullout bed. I've only slept on it twice and have had to take long, hot showers the next morning to loosen up the ache in my back, but Stephanie thinks Selma will be okay being as light as she is. Selma assures us she'll be fine. We leave her alone dreamily looking at my books.

Sliding underneath the covers with Stephanie, I shake my head. Over the years Selma's little threat that first night on Coventry Drive has faded a bit in my mind. I have, after all, married Stephanie and made her as happy as I know how. So there's been no reason to carry out any punishment against me. Still, the whole episode has left me feeling cracked open, exposed, as if Selma could see into places where I had never dared to look. It is unnerving. I have always hoped that a little part of Selma thought of me with something other than suspicion. Tonight, for the first time, it may have been there.

But the moment I let that idea float in, I remember Selma's tone and timbre, that world-weary dismissal from all those years ago. *You seem like a nice enough boy.*

"At least she made it here safe and sound," I say to Stephanie.

"Safe, yes," she says, "though maybe not so sound."

"Well, as you've been saying—insisting, actually—we're going to do our best to show her a good time, let her forget her troubles for a while."

Stephanie takes a couple moments to fluff up her pillow and arrange the covers over both of us—a nightly ritual. It seems that there will not be any recriminations from earlier.

"First Margaret and now Selma," Stephanie says. "How many of us are going to manage to fuck up our lives?"

At least it's a small blessing that she doesn't seem to include herself among the ranks of the wayward and derailed. I turn onto my side and give Stephanie a kiss goodnight. I can taste the slivovitz on her lips and, for just a second, I consider snuggling close and touching her. But then I think, no. Some days just need to end, and this one has that feel to it. I push my hand down and find Stephanie's under the covers. She gives it a little squeeze. Then she reaches over and turns out the light. It is always one of my favorite moments, those first few seconds when darkness floods the room, velvety and calm. And that's how I let it end, my eyes closing, the apartment and my wife familiar, until sleep takes me.

Four

Pondělí. A pleasant sense of purpose and possibility—and a momentary escape from Stephanie and Selma. Morgan has already opened the shop, started the engine, so to speak, of our little enterprise.

"Our fearless leader graces us with his presence," he says from behind the front counter, his Irish accent doing something wonderful with "graces," so that the word sounds very much like what it's supposed to mean. Morgan McBride has been in Prague longer than I have, longer, in fact, than Anthony or any of our friends, excepting Michael of course. No one is quite sure what his reasons were for leaving Ireland, but no one is pressing him very hard either. He simply reminds all who will listen of the long, long list of Irish expatriates, and Prague, he insists, is the new Paris—even if he is only an ersatz Joyce.

Morgan beckons me to hurry to the counter, where a package is unwrapped in front of him. "It's just arrived," he breathes. The Borges. I have owned this shop for four years and worked in a handful of others for more than half a dozen years before that, and still, the little prickling thrill never fails to come over me when a new book or manuscript arrives in the mail. There are gradations, of course, and I prefer books over the archival pleasures of manuscripts. Nevertheless, what's arrived this morning is enough to send any real bibliophile over the fucking moon. It is the original manuscript of Jorge Luis Borges's short story "Aleph," written in Buenos Aires in 1945. Most days, most booksellers will tell you that they are tradesmen. If you get them in a particularly cynical frame of mind they might even refer to themselves as blue-collar workers—"bricklayers," I once heard a particular burned-out man say. And, it's true: The moving around, the endless arranging and rearranging of often heavy tomes can bleed a bit of the romance from the work. But with a manuscript like this one, well, everything changes.

Sixteen pages of the master's story manuscript, written in his small, neat hand. Each individual page sealed in its very own plastic sleeve. According to Borges's protégé, Alberto Manguel, who read to the increasingly blind writer in his final years, the story was dedicated to Estela Canto, an Argentine writer to whom Borges had been romantically linked. In the story, the Aleph is the place in which all places have been assembled. The entire universe in the space of only a few centimeters. A place where everything exists together at once.

That this manuscript should have washed up in Prague, and so quietly, instead of being listed in a Sotheby's or Christie's catalogue, is a surprise. Some believe its value to be nearly $40,000.

And so, Morgan says, "There must be something wrong with it. I just haven't been able to figure out what it is."

"I'm not a Borges expert," I say, "but I think the manuscript is in order. If I had to guess, though, it's the provenance that's the problem."

Nevertheless, Morgan molds his hands around the edges of the pages reverently. Morgan: his hair buzzed tight against his scalp. Morgan: his round tortoiseshell glasses. Morgan: his thin, muscular body that always looks coiled and ready to spring into action. Morgan is not straight, though he is not absolutely gay either. Stephanie is convinced that he is in love with me, and there is a kind of lustful charge between us that Morgan likes to remind me of every so often—especially when he gets excited about our little biblio-triumphs. I've often let myself consider whether or not I had the impulse in me, tried to imagine what it would be like to have sex with a man—this man in particular. But every time I try, my imagination simply comes up empty. Still, I think he'd be an ironic and affectionate lover. I can easily imagine that cheery Irish pessimism, the alcoholic camaraderie, the smell of cigarettes on his clothes and hands.

"Thien Diep called just before you arrived," Morgan says, shaking himself out of his Borges revelry.

"You didn't mention the Borges to her, did you?"

"Of course not."

Good. Thien Diep is without a doubt my best client. One of my biggest surprises upon moving to Prague was the presence of such a large and vibrant North Vietnamese community. One doesn't think about travel and immigration between Cold War communist countries, but here are the Vietnamese, running restaurants and convenience stores all over the city. Thien Diep's husband is a particularly successful entrepreneur whose crowns have allowed her to forget all about her humble beginnings. Luckily for me, she has decided that modernist literature in English is the best way to communicate her new wealth to the world. She lives in a big hillside house near Kutna Hora where she entertains her friends with literary soirees and champagne. I like Thien. She is tough, but intelligent and considerate, and has a desire to live a life that is surrounded by books. A literary life, it used to be called. However, I don't want her to know about the Borges. She has decided that she is my special client and doesn't like to hear about me working on things outside of her interests.

An image of Thien and her literary protégés fills my mind. I can see her: short, smiling, her neatly cut hair spiked up like a punk rock idol or hidden beneath some kind of African-looking kofia, her living room filled with cigarette-smoking friends, nearly all Asian. Perhaps a young woman will soon be delivering a reading—her friends are almost always thin, intense-looking young women—and so has a manuscript clutched in one hand and a champagne flute in the other. In the corner is a gleaming grand piano where one of Thien's nieces is playing 1920s radio favorites.

"She said you should call her back if you can condescend to spare her a few minutes," Morgan says. "I think she was joking."

"So she's decided to sell her *To the Lighthouse.*"

"I don't think it can be anything else."

Most collectors have a theme, an idea around which they base their purchases. For Thien, her particular obsession is Blooms-bury. It is, I think, a satisfying niche. There's a fair amount out there and, of course, they were a particularly lively group. The books themselves are also very beautiful, many of the Hogarth Press covers designed and painted by Vanessa Bell.

Thien's *Lighthouse* is perfectly lovely, but there is a discol-oration on the back of her copy and an inscription, which she doesn't like. Unfortunately, with the downturn, this is probably not the moment to sell. Something Thien will not want to hear.

"Everything else has been quiet here," Morgan says. "How was your weekend? Mrs. Marten's birthday party? The neck-lace?" Somehow he manages to correctly make the word necklace sound lascivious.

"It went off perfectly. Maria Fuentes dedicated her reading to Stephanie."

"Wow."

"Yes, you know what weight that woman can give to a word. Dripping, I'd say, with sincerity. I think Stephanie actually blushed. And, of course, she loved the necklace."

"Of course."

"Fuck you, Morgan," I say, and we laugh. "But there's something else."

"This sounds serious."

"Maybe it is. Anna Nemcova is broke *and—*" I say, raising a palm and forestalling his shocked interruption, "and she plans to sell the Nemec family library to make up for it."

"She wants us to handle it?"

"Yes, indeed."

"Shit," Morgan says. "What the hell happened?"

"I don't know exactly. Michael offered some story about her uncle's bad investments in a Russian natural gas scheme. It wasn't very clear."

"Jesus, I bet that wasn't easy for Michael to admit."

"Probably not. His generally drunken state helped, though."

"Heh, good old Michael," Morgan says. "A right smart rummy. Are we happy?"

"Happyish."

"All right, boss. Tell me what I don't know. Unless I misunderstand you, we're in line to make a tidy sum."

"No, you understand it right."

"Well, then? Michael doesn't expect you to move the books for nothing, does he?"

"No, it's nothing like that. In fact, he was very clear that I should profit from his business." I pause to give Morgan a look. "I just wish I didn't have to."

"I'll not stand in your way of a little pro bono work," Morgan says. "I'd have thought you already knew that."

"I do, Morgan, and you're a great friend for it. The problem is Michael. He wouldn't like it if he thought I was giving him charity. Even for Anna's sake."

"Well." Morgan sighs and begins to pace behind the counter, a look of intense incredulity on his face. This is the kind of moment where Morgan would tell me that Michael is nothing but a "silly ass" and the devil with friends who won't accept help when they're in need. Surprisingly, though, he refrains from actually saying as much.

Instead, he says, "Well. Just think about the books that might be in such a collection. I know you have, no matter how you're feeling about Michael. I'll fucking bet you, I'll just bet you, there's a first edition *Mein Kampf* on those shelves."

And for a few minutes we begin to fantasize about the titles, the hidden treasures, that old Uncle Nemec has buried in Brno.

"*A Man Without Qualities.*"

"*The Quiet American.*"

"Something by James Baldwin."

"How about a pristine copy of *Orlando* for Ms. Diep?"

"Perfect."

"I'm getting a fucking erection just thinking about it," Morgan says.

"You better go do some work then," I say. "You never know when a customer is going to come in and interrupt you."

"Aye."

We are both laughing as Morgan goes to create a new display in our front window and I gather up the Borges manuscript and head back to my tiny office, the fantasy of the Nemec library still spinning happily in my head.

The office is there as I left it. Stacks of books lined up against three walls, a cramped desk with half a dozen Levenger fountain pens that I love almost as much as I love the books, newspaper clippings of book reviews going yellow at the edges, an old-fashioned Rolodex, a silver framed portrait of Stephanie when she was fifteen standing spindly-legged beside the family border collie, the chocolate tin filled with dirt from the grave of Rabbi Judah Loew ben Bezalel. In one corner there stands, like an anchor, a ten-thousand-pound, three-drawer filing cabinet with all of our little operation's important papers (and a bottle of Johnnie Walker Black). Carefully, I clear a space on the desk for the Borges manuscript and pour myself a cup of coffee from the thermos I've brought from home.

I stand in the doorway between my office and the main room and watch Morgan work. Every month that goes by, every important sale made, I grow more and more content with my little world. Look at this place. Smell it. A long table in the middle of the floor and six cases. Every inch of space accounted for. Perhaps two thousand books. Between us, Morgan and I could probably name every title, every author, and for the truly rare books, the narrative behind the book's life. It's a strange knowledge, maybe, not so obviously useful like surgery or auto repair or baking bread, but full of other gratifications. People, I've decided, need spaces to inhabit. The Hades is mine. Sometimes I actually believe that I could close my eyes and let my fingers play along the spines of the books, all fiction or literary biography here, and the stories would leap like light from the pages, travel up my arm, and into the deeper places of my body and fill me with a kind of power. It's a romantic idea, and not one I generally spread around, though I know Morgan understands it without our ever talking about it. Perhaps that's why Selma wants to come here? Life has hollowed her out, scoured her down to the last place before breaking, a thinness, a brittleness (how fragile those bones seemed when I held her), and she needs something, these narratives perhaps, to fill her up again.

Or maybe, Henry, she needs her husband to be released from prison.

I take a few sips of my coffee and resolve to get down to work. I'll have to do some thinking about the Borges. It's possible that the manuscript should go to Christie's regardless of where the current owner acquired the text. Or I'll put the word out to my dealer friends—some astute collector will understand its value. In fact, Borges is so white-hot right now I might be able to put together my own private auction. But these decisions should never be arrived at too quickly, and so I turn my attention to last week's project. The Fitzgerald came to me through an estate, as so many of our books do. Bibliophiles are often strange and secretive people, perhaps because they are misunderstood. Many prefer their books to the people in their lives and so, when the aging collector finally succumbs to the ravages of time or poor health, those who inherit their collections often have no clear idea of the value of the books in their possession. It would be an easy matter to discover the value, but you'd be surprised at the number who don't bother. And so, I am in possession of a beautiful presentation copy of F. Scott Fitzgerald's *The Beautiful and Damned*, New York:

Charles Scribner's Sons, 1922. Octavo, modern full crushed blue morocco gilt, elaborately gilt-decorated spine, raised bands, watered silk endpapers, all edges gilt.

It is, of course, a first edition, first issue, an exceptional presentation/association copy whimsically inscribed by Fitzgerald to his friend and fellow author Hyatt Downing, *"For Father Hyatt Downing S.D., A.P.A. P.H.D., T.A.B., S.O.L., D.D. O.K. Especially O.K. from F. Scott Fitzgerald, St. Paul March 2nd."*

I have listed it on our website at $20,000. For five weeks I've owned the book, read it by turning the pages with a tiny pair of wooden tongs, inspecting each page for flaws or distinguishing marks, and researched the relationship between Downing and Fitzgerald so that I could help create a narrative around this copy. I've found that collectors love a narrative—it's almost essential. And although he doesn't know it yet, I already have a buyer in mind. He's a Swiss who is living in San Sebastian hoping to—what?—channel the spectral energies of the Lost Generation. In any case, this is just his kind of thing.

Some books, like the Fitzgerald, have obvious markets. It's a relief sometimes to have what I call a *Field of Dreams* moment. "Build it and they will come." Acquire the book, prep it a little, determine a baseline price, photograph it for the website, write a little narrative, and presto! Even if the Swiss doesn't want it, someone will come forward. Two months from now, six months, eventually the book will move. The hard work comes with books whose value has been obscured by a fall in the author's reputation or, occasionally, when I have a hunch that a reputation will soon emerge. It's a little bit like playing a futures market: which books will quickly increase in value after only a few years, whose names will break through the growing tide of silence about contemporary literature and surface into consumer consciousness enough to turn a $27 book into a $600 one in only a few years' time. Even so, it doesn't take a genius to know the real money is there to be made with the Fitzgerald and the Borges rather than with the O'Nan, the Eggers, or even the Chabon.

What I should admit, though, is that this business is never likely to make me rich. Sometimes I pretend otherwise, but I know I'm only pretending. One year's crowning achievement is always eaten away by the next year's bear market. No, the true riches lie in working with these objects—artifacts, one critic friend has taken to calling them—that have the ability to change people's lives, to affect our hearts and minds, to link us with a past that we are always forgetting. No, even that sounds stuffy. What was C.S. Lewis's line? *We read to know we're not alone.* And I never, never feel alone when I'm in this little bookshop with all of these companions. I love the boards, the binding, the texture of the pages, the smell of dust and of the oil from past readers' hands. I love the epigraphs, the occasional illustration, even the choice of font, especially as it changes from era to era. And, for those who share this obsession, the endless hours of conversation that books engender make life worth living.

But just as I have taken my first sip of coffee, I hear the bell on the door chime and Morgan's voice welcoming someone. For some reason, I have to look, the person's voice hovering just on the edge of recognition. Ah, yes, Vincenzo DiBenadetto.

Another regular, so to speak. Forever browsing, but rarely buying. And a talker of almost Olympian abilities. I swear that there is a Vincenzo in almost everyone's life. Or, at least, everyone deserves one—if only to appreciate my pain. The man will talk and talk and talk, and his questions, while not stupid ones, become painful after you've answered them for the fifteenth time. What does a.e.g. mean? What's the difference between "good" and "fine"? If Vincenzo were a beautiful woman, no problem. Unfortunately, Vincenzo is seventy-seven years old (he tells us every time), always wears the same pair of corduroy trousers and olive button-down shirt, and has halitosis. He is from Abruzzi. Something else he always reminds us of. What he's doing in Prague I have always been afraid to ask. Today, he is Morgan's problem.

I need to call Thien Diep. Instead, I call the Swiss. Peter Bechtsold. His secretary answers. She has a sweet voice, and because we've never met, I have this perverse notion that she is fifty years old and bottle-blonde, like the stereotype of a phone sex worker. A face for radio. Her name is Amelia. "Hi, sweetheart, it's Henry Marten. Yes, that's right. The book dealer. I'm wonderful. And you? Good, good. Listen, will you give a message to Peter for me? Great. Tell him I have a book he's going to be really interested in. A Fitzgerald. No, not a *Gatsby*. *The Beautiful and Damned*. It's a wonderful copy. Tell him I have it on the website, and I'd be happy to answer any questions he might have. Okay, Amelia. You're a darling. You have a wonderful day, too. Bye."

I hate the telephone, and on some deep psychic level I find

these kinds of conversations exhausting. But it's done. Peter will look at the website. A Fitzgerald will be irresistible.

Then it's a string of emails to other dealers: Carl at Bauman's, Sophie at Bartleby's, Andrew at Maggs Bros., and Otto and Liesel at Saint George's. The emails, of course, are much simpler. Perhaps for everyone. It's possible that all I'll get are congratulations on acquiring such a fine book. But then it will live in their minds: Henry has a Fitzgerald. The network is both large and yet surprisingly small. Some days I feel as if I know everyone. Later, I'll include the Fitzgerald in the monthly newsletter that goes out to my subscribers.

The phone rings. "Hades Rare Books."

"Ah, so you decided to come to work today after all." Thien Diep.

"Hi, Thien. How are the bones?" This is my reference to All Saints Chapel, what many just call the "Bone Church." In the wake of a plague or a war or some other catastrophe, the monks of the church, led by Frantisek Rint, dug up the bones of thousands from the churchyard in order to make room for the new dead. Unsure of what to do with the exhumed remains, the monks decided to turn them into art: chandeliers made of femurs, miniature fountain-like sculptures using rib cages, arm bones, digits, tall pyramids of skulls so carefully worked together that only the precision of their own arrangement keeps them in place. For some reason, I'm fascinated that Thien has chosen to make her home nearby to this macabre museum and so tease her about it nearly every time we talk.

"I'm sure they are much as they've been for the last seven

hundred years," she says. "You know, Henry, I think you've developed an unhealthy obsession."

"No doubt," I say. "But you haven't called to talk about bones."

"No. Though I'm sure that you and Morgan have already thoroughly discussed my needs."

"We do have our suspicions."

"Then let's not waste any more time being cute."

"Right. You want to sell *To the Lighthouse*."

"I do."

"Thien, we've done a lot of business together, had many, many wonderful conversations. Frankly, you're one of the best book people I know. May I advise you?"

"After all that flattery I don't see how I can stop you."

"Good. Hold on to that Woolf. If you put it on the market now, you're going to lose money."

"Are you trying to tell me that political unrest in Libya has devalued my *Lighthouse*?"

"Something like that."

"Henry, I don't believe it. And even if I did, I simply don't care. Besides, I have absolute faith in you."

"I truly appreciate that."

"Do you know what I want?"

"Tell me."

"I want you to come get the book and work your magic. Photograph it, put it up on your website, tell the story of its inscription just as you've done with that Fitzgerald you put up last week. I know it will sell."

"I know it will too, Thien. But for thousands less than you paid for it."

"How many thousands?"

"At least two thousand."

"Come get the book."

"You know I'll be happy to do that, but if you don't mind telling me, what's the sudden hurry to get rid of it?"

"Our group is meeting in a month and I want something new to show them. We have some new members joining us, *new blood*." Thien then mentions to me the names of two fairly famous Asian-American writers who are visiting Prague in July as part of a conference held every summer at Charles University.

"That's very exciting, Thien. Are they collectors, too?"

"If they're not, they will be when I get through with them!" Thien lets out a loud cackle and I laugh along, too. It's easy to laugh when there's so much money to be made.

"Look, I know the Fitzgerald isn't your thing exactly, but it's impressive as hell."

"No. It's not Bloomsbury. Maybe if it were a *Gatsby*, but I loathe those two early books, especially *The Beautiful and Damned*. It's like soft-core pornography—boring as hell."

"Ha, ha, ha. Hey, Thien, tell me what you really think, okay?"

"Don't I always?"

"You do," I say. "Okay, very soon I'm going to Brno to look at a new estate. Do you know Michael Leo?"

"The Globe?"

"That's him. His wife is Czech and she's recently inherited a

large collection of English-language books. Morgan and I have
a hunch there's going to be something there for you."

"Oh, God, that would be wonderful, Henry."

"No promises."

"Of course not."

"I'm still making arrangements for when we'll go out there,
but why don't I come to Kutna Hora and pick up your Woolf
on the way? Unless you're prepared to trust it to the mails?"

"Never."

"I know, I'm just kidding. Why don't I call you back when I
know my plans for Brno?"

"That sounds lovely."

"Great. It's a date."

"Call me soon. I hate waiting for you to call me."

"I'll do it."

"Bye, Henry."

"Bye."

There are some days when you can smell, *smell* a big sale in
the making. As I hang up the phone, that old familiar scent is
in the air. A part of me thinks that Thien Diep is a ridiculous
human being. The problem is not her desire to collect books,
a thing I understand perfectly. But I've seen her copy of *To
the Lighthouse* and it's lovely. I couldn't imagine wanting to
get rid of it. Maybe it's just the hopelessly middle-class boy in
me who would never do anything at the loss of $2,000. What
I know is that I'll never give voice to these complaints because
Thien can do something that I cannot. Her soirees, as she calls
them, her little group of Asian bibliophiles, are priceless. Thien

will spend her crowns on something new, and unless I radically overestimate her, so will these new members. Perhaps it will not be a $20,000 Fitzgerald, but I can easily see a $350 Eugenides changing hands and eventually flying first-class back to America. So God bless Thien Diep and every bibliophile even remotely like her.

If I'm going to play the hero to Thien, then I think the Nemec Library is my best hope. The problem, of course, is that I'm totally ignorant of the collection or of the tastes of its owners. Who was this dead aunt of Anna Nemcova's? Did she love fiction? Poetry? Am I going to find four thousand useless Book-of-the-Month Club titles? Not likely, but my total ignorance is annoying. They can't possibly be intellectuals. If they were, the communists would have rooted them out and sent them to work in a mine somewhere. Scenes of Milan Kundera's Tomas, a brain surgeon, washing windows play through my mind. It would have been no easy trick to be an "old" family in the Czech Republic. Maybe they were sympathizers and struck deals with the Soviets to be left alone? It's the tidbit of the Russian natural gas deal that has me thinking like this. All bullshit, no doubt, straight out of a half-baked Cold War thriller. In any case, please let there be something for Thien. One tiny little Bloomsbury.

Also, there will be no harm in the books coming from Anna's family. Thien's new writer friends will probably also know of the Globe and appreciate the story of the book's origin. My dream: an English book, acquired from a wealthy Czech family, by an American book dealer (assisted by an Irishman), and sold to a North Vietnamese collector, who uses it to woo Chinese-American writers. I love it. That's Prague. I pray for this outcome the way a ten-year-old prays to kick the winning goal in soccer, with fervor and a heart full of innocence. And also a little fear. For all I know, Thien's got six other dealers out there looking for her next big purchase.

Time, then, to get moving. Call Anna. It's going to be horrible no matter how I do it. No one wants to publicize the moment they've stumbled, especially a woman as fiercely proud and intelligent as Anna Nemcova. Still, make the call. Be cheerful. She'll feel better when there's money in her hand.

"Anna!"

"Ah, Henry," she says. She sounds fine, absolutely fine. "How's Stephanie? Did she adore her party?"

"Of course she did. Everything was perfect. Thank you so much."

"You're welcome."

"Look," I say, "I spoke to Michael yesterday about your books."

"Oh, yes. The books." She's silent for a moment, though I hear her take in a breath as though she's going to speak. "You don't waste any time."

"The town where I come from, procrastination is a sin." I'm keeping my voice as jokey as possible. "Besides, better to have this over with as soon as possible."

"Is that what Michael told you?"

"No, actually. He didn't say that much. I guess I'm just speaking from experience."

"I'm sure you're right."

"If I've called in error, Anna, I'm sorry. All you have to do is say the word and it will be like we've never spoken today."

"No, you were right to call. I'm sorry." She presents me with a long, exaggerated sigh. I smile, that's Anna. "How do we start?"

"The first step is to catalogue the collection, see what you've actually got. Then I can work up an estimated value and make a plan for how to dispose of them."

"That's such a horrible phrase, Henry."

"What?"

"Dispose of."

"For book lovers, there are often no pleasant words to describe the selling of a book."

"Still, for someone who claims to love books, as you do, maybe you should come up with one."

I decide to pretend that this is a joke and laugh kind of faux heartily. "I'll work something up by the end of the day. How does that sound? But in the meantime, I can get to work if you'll give me your uncle's number. I can call him and agree on a time to evaluate the collection."

"Fine," she says. "That will be acceptable. I will have him call you before the end of the day."

And with that, she is gone.

For a moment, I sit there with the receiver in my hands until I realize that I'm holding my breath. Finally, I begin to fuss about with my fountain pens. I fill each one with new ink, carefully, like a science experiment, wipe them off with a cloth, play with their arrangement in the cup I use to keep them. After careful consideration, I select a pen and write out a fuller description of the Fitzgerald for the newsletter. I take my time, carefully flipping through the book for quotations to pull out that will establish the flavor of the novel. It is one of my favorite parts of the job, and I savor it like a delicious candy in the mouth— not chewing, but letting the sweet melt on my tongue until it's finally gone. When the description is finished, I pour myself yet another cup of coffee and swivel around in my desk chair, looking at the room and thinking.

The phone rings and I let Morgan answer it. For a while, I sit and listen to his voice in the other room. I breathe. I think vaguely of Selma's face in that moment when she was weeping in my wife's lap, the look of horror and mortification when she knew that I had seen her like that. Our laughter later. Then I find myself wondering what she's doing. Sleeping, I hope. Recovering from her journey. I close my eyes and try to see her sleeping. She is lying on her side, wrapped snug in the blankets Stephanie gave to her last night before we all went to bed, her own breathing peaceful, and strands of her dark hair spilled across her face and caught in the corner of her mouth.

Suddenly, I decide not to wait for Anna's arrangement and turn on the computer. It is a big, hulking monstrosity of a desktop. I find that I like old computers in the same way that I like old books. Eventually, its creaking machinations bring me to the Internet and I begin a search on Milos Nemec in Brno. There is very little to find, which is often the case with men of his generation, but there is a telephone listing. I mark down the number and pick up the phone. The line rings and rings and rings. It is such a normal part of modern life that some kind of answering machine or voicemail should be prepared to record my communication that I am surprised when I realize that the phone has continued to ring long after any reasonable expectation that it will be answered.

Then I hear the bell on our door jingle several times and feel the presence of tourists and their money coming from the other room. For another hour I go out and help Morgan with the customers. I sell to an American father and his ten-year-old son a first edition of *The Hobbit*. The dust jacket is of the original design, but the copy is from the eighteenth printing. Still, a very nice sale at $300. When the father gives the book to the boy, his big brown eyes widen even further. I tell him to open the book and place his nose between the pages.

"Take a deep breath," I say. "Do you smell it?"

The boy nods. "What is it?" he wants to know.

"Time," I say. "That's what it smells like."

The father and I laugh, but as they're walking away, the boy keeps turning back to look at me, and I have this feeling, one that creeps up the back of my neck, that he will remember this moment for the rest of his life.

At lunchtime, I go for a walk and surprise myself by stopping at a street vendor and buying a sausage sandwich that I cover in creamy yellow mustard. I look around at the crowds of people and the bright blue sky. Another line from Henry Miller leaps into my mind: "The day began gloriously." I say it aloud to test the way it sounds in the Czech air. "The day began gloriously." I look at the crowds schlepping their way up the hill to the castle and then schlep my own way back to the Hades.

It is Morgan's job to check the shop's email for Internet sales in the morning and it is my job after lunch. There is a message from Peter Bechtsold:

Re Fitzgerald. HAVE FREED MYSELF TO TRAVEL TO PRAGUE NEXT WEEK. WILL PHONE WHEN I ARRIVE. HOLD THE FITZGERALD.

Build it, I think, and they will come.

I have just wandered out from the office to tell Morgan about Bechtsold's visit when Anthony blows through the front door dancing like Fred Astaire. "Good morning," he sings, "good *morning.*" Anthony is not usually this chipper, and journalists have a reputation for hard-boiled cynicism and dry ironic humor to uphold. Something, some story, must be very good indeed.

Anthony takes up his traditional seat on a high stool behind the counter and because it's after 1 PM I offer him a scotch. As soon as he's settled with his glass, he begins.

The Senate is meeting once again to discuss the issue of allowing an American missile defense system on Czech soil. The missiles themselves won't actually be here, they'll be in Poland or maybe Bulgaria, but the radar systems will be here. The Czechs had said no to the Americans, and I thought the topic was dead. In fact, for once, the Czechs were very happy with their government's response. But now the issue seems to have been revived. So it's already been a good news day. Even more importantly, I discover that a very beautiful (and available) *New York Times* reporter is in town and that Anthony has secured a date for dinner. This is not the first "dinner date" he's had with this woman and he's very excited for the evening. Morgan and I have already heard the stories from her last visit to Prague.

While I'm listening I find myself wanting to tell Anthony about Anna Nemcova, tell him the whole business: the financial trouble, the collection in Brno, the unfortunate telephone conversation from the morning. We are all friends, I reason. Perhaps Michael has already told Anthony himself. But eventually discretion wins out and I mostly sit and listen to Anthony's morning.

"Maybe you'd like to bring Selma out with us tonight?" he says.

I had mentioned that Selma was coming to visit us, but only in passing, and Anthony had not seemed to really be paying attention. This sudden invitation surprises me.

"I was thinking of going to U Sudu," he says.

"She might have fun."

"Don't you think we'll be in your way?"

"Well, not to be too crass about it, Belinda is pretty much a sure thing."

For reasons I can't quite explain, something doesn't feel right. Something in Anthony's voice. The way he looks into his drink when he talks.

"Part of Selma's idea in coming to Prague was to escape her troubles, you know? I'm not sure if having dinner with two American journalists, especially one from New York, is much of an escape."

"Why don't you ask her and see what she says?"

Is Anthony pushing? I have a tremendous respect for Anthony's ability to manipulate a situation. This is how he makes his living, getting people to tell him things they probably didn't wake up in the morning wanting to divulge. Though for the life of me I can't imagine what his angle might be. If he even has an angle. Nor can I explain this sudden protectiveness I feel about Selma. Maybe, at long last, I'm finally developing a nose for trouble. On the other hand, maybe I need to take a sip from my scotch and relax.

Ah, Anthony, you asshole. Complicating my life.

"I'll definitely ask her," I say, forcing a full measure of levity into my voice. "You're right, it could be fun. Stephanie loves U Sudu."

"Wonderful."

"Of course," Morgan says, "no one has thought to invite me."

We laugh and pretend to beg his forgiveness. His response is unrepeatable. Then Anthony finishes his drink and we walk together onto the sidewalk to say good-bye. Now that he's made his invitation, Anthony seems in a hurry to go. Fred Astaire has disappeared. We shake hands and I try to make him look me in the eye. Something he won't do for more than a second. Okay, Anthony.

It's hard not to think of Anthony. I find I'm already calling it the Anthony Interlude, as if it were a chapter in a French novel. Something from Dumas, perhaps, that will lead to political intrigue and a sword fight. Eventually, I think, *Fuck it.*

While I'm still shaking off Anthony's visit the phone rings again and Morgan is saying, "Yes, sir. He is in, sir. Just one moment." Then with his hand over the receiver, "It's Uncle Nemec."

I'm impressed with what could possibly have transformed Morgan into a machine of polite subservience. I raise an eyebrow as I take the phone.

"Henry Marten."

"Mr. Marten, this is Milos Nemec. I believe you know my niece." The English is slow and precise, but there's absolutely no hint of uncertainty.

"I do indeed," I say. "Thanks so much for calling."

"It's my pleasure."

There's a slightly awkward moment when no one says anything, and I realize that it's my job to drive us through this awkward business. I have not considered what Milos Nemec's attachment may be to the books.

"Well, we're honored to be of service to you. I truly value my friendship with Michael and Anna."

Nemec does not actually answer this with words but instead offers a kind of grunt. Disconcerting.

"Our first step in (I almost say "disposing of") moving the books for you is to make an accurate catalogue of the collection. Do you know how many there are?"

"Several thousand, I should think. The books represent the family's interests over nearly 150 years."

"I was told that the most recent custodian of the books was your wife?"

"Yes."

"Well, here is what I'm thinking. I'm making a trip east later this week, on Wednesday. If it's acceptable to you, I can arrive on Wednesday afternoon, perhaps do a little preliminary work and then return on Thursday morning to really create the catalogue. Depending on the number of books, I think this early work can be finished in one day."

"I think that will be fine."

"Terrific. I wonder if you can recommend a hotel that's close to your home?"

"I'd be very happy to invite you to stay with us at the house," Nemec says. "Wouldn't that be more convenient?"

"That would, absolutely. It's very kind of you to invite me. I'll probably have an assistant with me as well."

"That's not a problem."

Nemec tells me the address of the home and gives me a phone number—not the same number I discovered online—and it seems that the conversation is winding down in the normal way.

"Mr. Marten?" Nemec says. "This is a very unpleasant business for us."

"I understand," I say.

"Good. I sense that maybe you do. If my Paulina were still alive, this would surely have killed her."

"Well," I say, "let's try to honor her memory by finding these books new homes with readers who will know how to appreciate them."

"Thank you."

"You're very welcome," I say. "Until Wednesday, then?"

"Good-bye, Mr. Marten."

"Good-bye, sir."

I find as I'm hanging up the phone that my hands are shaking. Suddenly I can understand the change that came over Morgan when he spoke to Milos Nemec. There's something about talking to that man. A sense that you've just had a conversation with the Past. But more than that. Here is a man who has never watched an episode of *South Park* or discussed the literary merits of comic books, who probably only has a television set to watch CNN or follow financial reports, a man whose life is gliding along at least briefly with mine, but who has never once considered the merits of various cleaning products for carpet stains.

And then. And then there are the books. It's clear to me that Nemec has no idea what he has in that collection and what he does not. A true bibliophile, even one who is being forced to sell off his collection, would not have failed to mention the cream of the crop, to gain at least one more ounce of conversational pleasure from what he has accumulated. No, this was his wife's work and if he cares about its disposal at all it is probably just the notion of loss that bothers him, that what was great has now been diminished. Still, all this is only part of the reason I'm keyed up. The rest is the books. What were Nemec's words? A hundred and fifty years of the family's interests. What might not be there? There could easily be Brochs or Musils or, heaven help me, Kafkas. Now, I think, who has the erection?

Intruding herself into the midst of my success fantasies is Selma.

"What did he say?" Morgan asks, interrupting my thoughts.

"What?"

"Old man Nemec. *What-did-he-say?*"

"Oh, right." I try to make a joke of my distraction. "I'm going out there on Wednesday after I visit Thien."

"Did he say anything about the books?"

"Very little." I lean with my back against the counter and fold my arms over my chest. "I'm going to stay at the house."

"Well, aren't we important."

"I'm excited to see the books," I say.

"Of course you are."

I suggest another drink and pour us both a finger of scotch. But even as we're drinking—something we do nearly every afternoon—I find myself staring out the window at the blue sky and people passing on the street.

"You feeling all right today, Henry?" Morgan says.

"Yes, I'm fine," I say. "It's my wife's friend Selma—she's staying with us. She is broken a little now, you know what I mean?"

"Yes."

"I'm worried about her. And though it's totally irrational, I have this idea that she's brought her troubles with her—like a disease I might catch. Stupid, I know."

"No," Morgan says, "it's not stupid at all. Remember, my friend, you're talking to an Irishman."

We laugh a little halfheartedly and finish our drinks.

"Why don't you go home and see her?" Morgan says. "Isn't Stephanie at the embassy?"

"Yes, Selma's on her own."

"What kind of host are you? Go entertain the woman. I can handle things here for the next couple of hours. Besides, this mood of yours is making me nervous."

"Really?"

"Yes! Go!"

I decide to walk home. I have only my coffee thermos with me and a first edition of A.S. Byatt's *Possession* that I plucked off the shelf on the way out the door. At the last minute I decide to make it a gift for Selma. The novel has so many things going for it: the page-turning qualities of a mystery, a brief dissertation on poetry, and of course, intertwining love stories. I have in my head a vision of Selma sitting with a steaming cup of tea and quietly reading.

I walk across the Charles Bridge and look at the vendors and the musicians and the tourists. A young Czech is singing a 1930s American blues standard. Couples kiss and hold hands while looking out at the gently moving Vltava. Children sit to have their caricatures drawn. On foot anyway, it's difficult not to feel as though you're being pulled into something powerful, an event whose gravitational pull might rival one of Jupiter's moons. It's only when I'm off the bridge and headed home toward the Jewish Quarter that I can refocus on Selma.

When I unlock the front door, the apartment is quiet and I feel vaguely disappointed that Selma has gone out. But then I listen more closely and can hear the sound of the shower running. I look at my watch and smile. 2:47. That would be a good sleep if it's what she's been doing. At the very least, a lazy morning. I walk into the study where the pullout bed now dominates the room, the sheets and blankets in a tangle, Selma's open suitcase on the floor beside it. Despite myself, I kneel down to look through it: the folded jeans, the T-shirts, the bras and panties that I linger over for a minute before forcing myself into more mature behavior. I find a Post-it note from my desk and write a message for Selma to find with the book. *Welcome to Prague!* I write. *Thought you might enjoy this one!* I linger over the note for a minute, vaguely unhappy with the exclamation points, but ultimately decide not to change anything. Just affix the note to the dust jacket and leave it on her pillow.

The shower is still going, and a fruity scent, maybe from Selma's shampoo, drifts underneath the door and into the hallway where I'm standing, unsure of what to do with myself. Perhaps I've drunk too much scotch. I feel suddenly the overwhelming need to lie down and go to the bedroom. I close the door quietly behind me and throw myself onto the bed. Close my eyes. As a child I was always comforted by the sounds of ambient noise. Dryers tumbling, the fans of space heaters endlessly oscillating, hair dryers, showers. I listen now and soon settle into a calm place. The bathroom is just on the other side of the wall and every once in a while I can hear Selma moving in the tub. I rest my arm across my eyes to block out the light. Oddly, my breathing settles and deepens at the same time that I become aware of the beating of my heart. And then, to my great surprise, I hear Selma begin to sing. I strain to understand the words until I realize that she's singing in Arabic. The melody is a gentle one, a lament, I think, maybe a love song. Her voice is clear, she could be in the room. Or I could be in there with her. And as soon as I let the idea in, I feel myself grow hard and my hand drifts down to touch myself. I can see her damp hair, her clean face scrubbed free of all makeup, the water gliding down and around the curves of her body, her eyes closed in her own private reverie as she sings. Unaware that I am so close, I tug and tug. When the release comes, I bite into the fabric of my shirt to keep the noise that escapes to a quiet growl.

Five

In Nabokov's novel *Lolita*, Humbert Humbert's first love was a young girl named Annabel. And as with so many first loves, his memory of it is indelible. It was a summertime love, and the girl-child was sweet and kind, but also shyly ready to discover her sexuality. In a secluded cove on the beach, with the sound of the ocean as a soundtrack to their afternoons, they touched and petted and kissed. Humbert knew for the first time the smell of a lover's skin, the painful softness of her hair, the invisible cocoon of quietude and stillness that can be created between two people who are wholly immersed in each other. When only a few months later the sweet Annabel contracts typhus and dies, their young love becomes burned into his memory, idealized and, according to Humbert, infects his every future desire. Because while he grows up and grows old, his idea of love never matures—to catastrophic effect.

It is always with Nabokov in mind that I remember my own first kiss.

When I was eleven years old, a new family bought the house across the street from ours. The Al-Juhanis were a family of three: Mother, Father, and a daughter my age named Dena. Dena was something of a tomboy. She had grass stains on her blue jeans and wore the same blouse in three different colors, blue, black, and white, every single day. She could run fast. She could beat me in arm wrestling. And she smelled regularly of tomato soup.

Even though Dena and I were neighbors, there was no particular reason why we should have become friends. In fact, we seemed to have very little in common and for months after she moved in only waved hello to each other when we passed on some errand in the company of our parents. And even that was just to demonstrate that we knew how to be polite. Indeed it was a very odd thing that brought us together.

I was going through what people usually call a *phase*. I had ceased to hang out with my friends after school to play baseball and football. I'd grown moody. I spent hours locked in my room with the door shut and a DO NOT DISTURB sign scrawled in the handwriting of an ax murderer and posted crookedly with Scotch tape. My parents began to wonder about me, though they needn't have worried. Because what I was doing behind that closed door was nothing perverse, nothing shocking, nothing yet shameful. I was reading, quite systematically, *The Complete Sherlock Holmes*. In fact, in just a few months' time I went from being a relatively normal boy to a Holmes aficionado. From my savings I purchased a reproduction Calabash pipe and a deerstalker hat. At a garage sale I bought a battered violin that was missing its bow and one of its strings. I "borrowed" a magnifying glass from the junk drawer in the kitchen. In the evening, armed with these accoutrements, I stealthily canvassed the neighborhood looking for clues and avoiding human contact. For a good long while I succeeded. It was Dena who eventually caught me out.

Dressed in my deerstalker and with the pipe clenched between my teeth, I was examining with my glass a set of animal tracks left in the fresh mud of an access lane that wound behind my house. I had just straightened up and turned to a wholly imaginary Watson and said, "Have a look here with this glass and tell me what you make of these tracks," when Dena slipped from her hiding spot among a stand of pine trees. It was immediately clear that while I had been tracking some unknown beast (a bunny rabbit in all probability), Dena had been tracking me. She came up to me, just as bold as you like, and took the magnifying glass from my hands to examine the tracks. When she turned again to face me—my cheeks glowing a bright fire-engine red—Dena said, "You know, Holmes, I believe those tracks were made by a hound. But look at the size of them! I have never in all my long experience seen the creature that could belong to those tracks, save maybe the wild tigers of Afghanistan." For a moment I simply stared at her, astonished. She was perfect—or, at least I thought so. The diction was a brilliant facsimile of the Holmesian idiom, the subtle reference to *The Hound of the Baskervilles* opened the door to hours of play, and the expert's knowledge of Dr. Watson's military service in Afghanistan demonstrated that I was in the presence of a soul mate. That afternoon, we ran together across fog-streaked moors, interviewed superstitious locals, and eventually shot the dreaded hound with Watson's service revolver. It was only as the sun began to set and I realized I was in all probability late for dinner that we introduced our real selves.

"I'm Henry Marten," I said.

"I know," she replied. "I'm Dena." And so it began.

The Al-Juhanis had a swing on their back porch that we pretended was a horse-drawn carriage that transported us from one side of London to another. The closed-in front porch of my house was the rooms at 221B Baker Street. We agreed without discussion that I would always play the part of Holmes. But Dena was a chameleon; she was Watson, Irene Adler and, when necessary, Professor Moriarty.

My first kiss then came unexpectedly, on a blustery November afternoon. I was sitting on the floor of our Baker Street rooms (the front porch), a thin and hawkish boy wearing a deerstalker cap. I had snuck a roll of wrapping paper and the Scotch tape from the closet in my mother's bedroom in order to wrap a gift I'd bought for Dena. I had discovered, using my now enhanced powers of deduction, that it was Dena's birthday. I thought I'd found the perfect gift. At the mall one afternoon with my mother, we'd passed a novelty shop with a T-shirt hanging in the front window that read DR. WATSON IS MY CO-PILOT. There was a disembodied deerstalker hat and, below it, a Calabash pipe floating at just about the place you'd expect a man's mouth to be. I knew immediately that this was the gift I wanted to give to Dena. When I told my mother why I wanted to buy the T-shirt, I watched her face—almost like a slot machine—processing all of the possibilities of the fact that I wanted to spend my hard-earned allowance on a present for a girl. Bewildered, she helped me select the correct size.

After taking this necessary help, I wanted to be entirely alone with my gift. I didn't want to talk about it; my mother, though she tried mightily, couldn't get me to speak another word about the shirt or about Dena. I refused any assistance in folding it or wrapping it. This enterprise, whether it turned out a smashing success or an utter failure, would be completely and entirely mine. Somehow, my father sensed this and, when he saw me moving out to the porch with the wrapping paper and the tape, had the good grace to say absolutely nothing.

The clerk at the mall had nicely folded the T-shirt and, though I almost desperately wanted to look at the graphics again, I didn't dare undo this work. I knew that I'd never get it folded quite so nicely again. So instead, I satisfied myself with taking in a deep breath of that chemical new shirt smell and brushing the black fabric against my cheek.

I had watched my mother wrapping Christmas and birthday gifts for years and so knew, in principle, how it was done. Unfortunately, I'd never actually wrapped anything myself. Mother had always wrapped my father's gifts from me and Father had always paid donations to the old ladies at the mall who set themselves up to do gift wrapping for charities. It turned out that there were important fine-motor skills involved in the wrapping of presents that I had never considered. On my first attempt, I failed to cut off enough paper so that as I centered up the shirt it was like trying to cover a giant with a baby blanket. I crumpled up that attempt and threw it into the imaginary Baker Street fireplace. I overcompensated on my next attempt and had so much paper that the ends were too thick to be held closed with mere Scotch tape. I decided then to untape those ends and cut away much of the excess. The problem was that I was like a drunk with those scissors, cutting the paper in waves and nicks. Eventually, I could at least say that the T-shirt was entirely covered in paper—even if the general shape of the present looked like something the cat might cough up.

Still, I'd done my best. I looked through a little bag of tags, the kind that say TO and FROM, and selected one that had pink balloons and streamers on it.

"Who is that present for?"

At the sound of her voice, I froze as though I'd been caught doing something much more illicit than wrapping a present.

"Hi, Dena," I said. "When did you get here?"

"Just now. Did I scare you?"

"No. You scare me? No."

I looked at Dena. Her face was wide with a grin, and her eyes looked big and liquescent. She wore a brown corduroy jacket over her white blouse.

"Whose birthday is it?" she asked.

"You know very well whose birthday it is," I said and dropped the unlabeled tag on top of the gift.

Dena kneeled beside me on the floor of the porch and poked the present the way you might poke the stomach of a teddy bear. "Could that," she said, "be a present for me?"

Why yes it could. Just a tiny, little rhetorical question. But the way that Dena asked her question—half innocent, half coy—created a painful mixture of emotions swirling in my head that left me feeling slow and dull, like a stroke victim. I had been caught being foolish, trapped in a gesture that was beyond my ability to pull off, a stupid and inept boy who wasted his life away reading books in his room while the wide world marched on, and who then dressed up in the clothing of his literary heroes to . . . to what? At the time I could not even have explained my intense desire to be something, anything, other than who I was. But then to be prematurely discovered by Dena engineering some hopeless act of adolescent affection. Such humiliations cannot be described.

Faced with the unhappy choice of leaping up, running into the house, and hiding for the rest of my life behind the locked door of my bedroom or finishing my gesture and giving Dena her gift, I picked up the clumsily wrapped T-shirt and held it out to her with both hands, a little like Oliver Twist offering his bowl to be filled with just a bit more soup. It seemed to take her forever to unwrap it. She was so careful to pull away each piece of tape, but eventually the T-shirt was in her hands and unfolded to reveal DR. WATSON IS MY CO-PILOT and the deerstalker hat and Calabash pipe. Dena smiled, but then did a strange and wonderful thing: She put the T-shirt up to her nose and took a deep long sniff of that new T-shirt smell and then gently rubbed the fabric against her cheek. That was the moment when I leaned in close to Dena and pressed my lips against hers and I felt her press back, and we stayed like that for two, three, four seconds. It was a wonderful moment, that first kiss, a silly, totally-without-expertise, no-style-whatso-ever kind of kiss. Still, in the twenty-five years that have passed since that day, I have never stopped being grateful.

In a way, I have been in love with the idea of Dena Al-Juhani from that moment until this one in Prague. Long before I knew that I wasn't unique, that Humbert's Annabel was waiting for me to discover her in Nabokov's book so that Dena could be transformed from adolescent love into adult preoccupation. As an adult, even happily married, I have thought to search for Dena a thousand times. It would be easy enough now with the Internet. If I was even a little lucky I might be able to see her face—her adult face—it might only take seconds. Imagine all those quiet moments in my office at the Hades, the computer already booted up, a search engine blinking or pulsing in the right-hand corner of the screen. Just waiting for me to type the letters of her name. Dena Al-Juhani. So far, I have been a coward, afraid of what I might find. Will I discover that she married some doe-eyed Arab boy? That she lives in Amman and has borne him two sons?

That what was a slight thickness around the middle as a teen-ager has turned into, well . . . you know? That she is not as well educated or ambitious or, frankly, glamorous as my wife? All of these things perhaps, and more, that I will not allow myself to know. Some fantasies should never be dispelled.

———

It feels strange to be lying in bed in the middle of the afternoon. Indolent. The only times I have ever done it were on vacation or during some childhood illness.

Watching the light shift along the wall or listening to muted sounds from the street where people are out living and working, I want very much to have never left the bookstore. It is so easy to know myself there. This other Henry, the one who gets off thinking about his wife's friends while they sing in the shower I know less well. I am not ashamed of him exactly—reading has taught me that there are so many ways to be human—but I would not want anyone to know this secret self.

Selma is out of the shower now, dressing, putting on perfume.

I am trying to come to terms with the clumsy psychology that links Dena to Selma. It's embarrassing, really, in its lack of subtlety.

No matter our age, there is always part of us that is a child waiting to be comforted. Though maybe we are too stupid to understand it this way. I try to think now of what comforts me. The way the light changes at dusk, the rhythms of my body halfway through a long run, the smell of an old book and the weight of it in my hand, dark wood like the stacks at my town's little library, clenching my teeth to the stem of my Calabash pipe, and Dena's features: the tone and color of her skin, her dark curly hair, her mannerisms and subtle accent, her precociousness. Yes, so many of the things that I loved about that girl are reproduced now, imperfectly, but reproduced nonetheless, in the form of Selma Al-Khateeb.

My mind is drifting, moving and shifting from place to place. Does any of this really matter?

Resting my arm over my eyes to block out the light, I find myself thinking of Selma as she was all those years ago on Coventry Drive. In matters of love she has become the face of my conscience: judge, jury, and executioner. How she would hate me for desiring her. That vicious voice, like venom, *ven-om-ous*, seeking out some soft place in the ear to infect me. I am made sick with the thought that I am a person whom someone could hate. And Selma, now that she is a figure of pity, now that her life has been shattered, bludgeoned really, is no longer relegated in my mind, no longer so absolutely defined by those few minutes on Coventry Drive when she warned me against hurting Stephanie. The danger is still there, but now coupled with something else.

I can hear Selma leaving her bedroom and walking briskly down the hall. Did she find the book I left her and read my note? Probably she's looking for me even now. Wondering if I am here. Wondering what to do. I zip up my pants in case she's brave enough to look in here. I prepare what I will say to her. Something about not wanting her to spend the whole day alone in a strange apartment in a strange city. All perfectly true.

Selma is probably in the living room now. I hear her pause,

then a softer silence. Sitting down somewhere. What is she thinking about? I want her to have normal thoughts just like any other guest in Prague. I want her to make plans for shopping on Paris Avenue or watching the changing of the guard at the castle or strolling along the Vltava until she reaches the throng of Charles Bridge. But I fear her thoughts are back in the States, in New Jersey. I'd bet money on it, in fact.

Faintly, I can hear her dialing a cell phone, then a pause, then Selma's voice.

I am straining, concentrating every ounce of energy into listening to what she says.

"This is Selma Al-Khateeb."

"A-l hyphen K-h-a-t-e-e-b."

"Yes, that's right."

"I really must speak to Mr. Sprecher. He told me he'd call today."

"Of course, I appreciate that."

"No. Tell Mr. Sprecher that he needs to appreciate—"

"Fine. Yes. Good-bye."

There is a deep pause, like waiting for thunder after a lightning strike. Then a loud crash. It takes me a moment but I realize Selma has thrown her cell phone against the wall.

Time to come out of hiding again, Henry Marten.

———

I stand, listening, with my hand on the knob of the bedroom door. I am trying to steady myself, arrange my face before I walk into the room and confront Selma. Whatever I do or say to her, I want it to be calm and graceful. I want to be reliable. Prague already makes me mysterious. I try to decide who she could have been talking to. Mr. Sprecher must be . . . a lawyer? Some government official? I had asked Selma if she had news of Mansour. Perhaps she had been trying to get some. Perhaps she calls Mr. Sprecher every day. And every day she is told the same thing: no new developments. They'll call her as soon as they know anything. Cold comfort for a woman whose husband has been locked away for more than a year. In my mind, I walk into the living room and pick up Selma's cell phone (it's still in one piece, nothing that can't be rubbed away with a shirtsleeve) and hand it to her. *C'mon, Selma, let's say we put our cares aside and go explore the city.* As if her cares were nothing more than jet lag or being three days late on paying her credit card bill. As if the city itself held some magic. And yet. Would this suggestion actually be a bad one, all things considered? Better, yes, to move out into the street, into the world, to look up at the bright sky and breathe the Central European air than to sit curled in the fetal position on my couch.

Enter then, stage right.

She is, indeed, on the couch with her legs stretched out before her. She is startled when I walk in, as I knew she would be. She does a kind of double-take and I watch her face go from surprise to a smile to resignation. All these expressions, so fast, that it's hard to credit the reality of any of them. "You're always sneaking up on me," she says, but there's no malice in the accusation.

"Good morning," I say.

"I can't believe how long I slept."

"It's good for you, just what the doctor ordered."

There's a turntable in the corner of the room, new, but built to look like an old Philco radio. I walk over and flip through some of our records. The room needs some music, something to build up its character, fill out the corners of the atmosphere. I select a Mozart concerto and carefully lower the needle on the record. Before we bought this Philco imitation I hadn't owned a turntable in years. Collecting old records has become a hobby that Stephanie and I share together. I explain this to Selma. How the act of lowering the needle onto the record, the scratch and hiss, makes me feel good.

"Do you think that's weird?" I say.

"No. But I didn't know you liked classical music."

"Like all things worth knowing, it's been an acquired taste," I say. "You'll discover you can't stay in Prague for any length of time and not get caught up in this music."

A few minutes pass as we listen to the Mozart and I think I can see a little bit of the tension bleed away from Selma. I suggest a cup of tea and she agrees. Selma stands with me in the kitchen and watches me prepare it. I take my time, using the good cups and saucers, filling the elegant creamer with milk and placing the whole business on a black lacquered Japanese tray that someone at the embassy gave Stephanie as a gift. There is the feeling of ritual to it. And between the tea and the music, these tiny markers of culture, the atmosphere in the apartment has altered. When Selma takes her first sip of tea, she gives a soft little moan and smiles. The physical pleasure of relief.

I haven't had to say anything, just play a little music and

make a little tea, and already Selma seems better. Morgan, God bless him, was right to send me home.

"That pullout bed didn't kill you, did it?" I say.

"No, it was fine. I loved sleeping in that room actually, surrounded by so many books."

"I know. Sometimes if I can't sleep I'll go in there and lie on the couch and just look at the titles."

"It's like they're standing on guard," Selma says. I just look at her.

"Talismans," I say. "That's how I think of them."

"Let's go look at them!"

We take our teacups into the study and I lean against my desk to watch her look through my books. Her fingertips play along the spines like a pianist creating a gentle flourish. It's a beautiful thing to watch someone's mind at work and, even though I have no way of knowing what she's actually thinking, I know perfectly the feeling of engagement and contentment that looking through a new collection can bring. For a second, I imagine the books of Milos Nemec and feel the spark of anticipation.

"Are these your private books?" Selma says. "Or is this just an overflow from the bookshop?"

"These are mine. The ones I tell myself I'll never sell." This makes her smile.

"Which ones are *the* books for you? The ones that have influenced your life the most."

"God, what a question." I try to laugh it away, but I can see that she wants an answer. I start to scan the shelves.

"Are they a secret?"

"No. If you had asked me that question at twenty-five I would have answered right away. No hesitation. But now there are so many . . ."

"Just pick some then. Three."

Because Michael had mentioned it on Sunday I pull out a boxed edition of Rostand's *Cyrano de Bergerac*, Somerset Maugham's *The Moon and Sixpence*, and Henry Miller's *Tropic of Cancer*. I surprise myself with the choices and try to decide what they say about me, because for what other reason could you possibly want to know what I'd select? I am happy because the story I think they tell about me is complex and contradictory. Especially the Rostand and the Miller. Who is the man who could endorse the radically divergent ideas of love found in those two books? Let Selma sort it out.

"Ugh, not that book!" she says, meaning the Miller.

I am not surprised. Few women seem to appreciate *Tropic of Cancer*. But I am a veteran of such moments and have my response prepared.

"It's been my experience that the only people who don't like Henry Miller are those who haven't actually read him."

"Guilty!" she says, and seems very happy about it. Then she looks at Maugham's book. "Why *The Moon and Sixpence*? I've never read it."

"It's a fictional account of the life of Paul Gauguin. Do you know his story?"

"He painted natives in Tahiti."

"He did indeed. But did you know that at thirty-five Gauguin decided to drop out of his own life in order to paint? He was

a stockbroker and married with two children, and one day he
more or less just up and left them to pursue his art."

"That's horrible. To leave your children like that."

"In a way, yes. But also courageous. I think that's why I like
the book so much. It's an expression of values."

"What values?" Selma asks a little incredulously.

"I'll give you the bumper sticker version: Art Before Babies."
As I say it, I spread my hands out in the air as though I'm
smoothing a bumper sticker onto the back of a car. I also smile
my most charming smile.

"I still think it's horrible."

"That's your right," I say.

I smile again and replace the books on their shelves. We
drink the rest of our tea, which is not quite cold. In a moment
I will ask Selma if she'd like to go out and find something to
eat. It will still be several hours before Stephanie gets home
and, in any case, we can call and tell her where to meet us. But
before I say this, before I suggest that we stick to the Jewish
Quarter tonight, to the lovely shopping and a drink later in the
Café Franz Kafka, I think that moments like this one, where
friendship and good feeling can be so swiftly undercut by just
a single false note, are what literature can do for us—render the
everyday and its painful complexities so perfectly. I am suddenly, terribly in love with my life, so much so that I want to
take Selma to the Hades right away and show her everything.
But I swallow my enthusiasm for the moment. Feed the girl
first, I tell myself. Show her the rest of your life later.

Six

Maybe something has changed in me, but as I walk beside Selma on the streets of the old Jewish Quarter, stopping by the Kafka statue to take a photo of Selma with her arm linked through his, I find that more than sex, what I want is to offer her an escape from her life. I look at her, so thin, so fragile-seeming — damaged, really — throwing her cell phone across the room in desperate frustration one moment and then having a conversation with me about Henry Miller the next. Maybe making her a cup of tea, going for a walk through this city, buying her a late lunch, I am discovering my best self.

"Let's keep walking," I say. "We must be flaneurs."

This word makes her laugh, and oddly blush, as if she thinks it too ridiculous a term to ever apply to herself. We will move together, one foot in front of the other, from neighborhood to neighborhood, restaurant to restaurant, architectural wonder to architectural wonder, and no one will weep or lie curled in the fetal position or think, for more than a few moments at a time, about incarcerated husbands, or politics, or America. The photo I take of Selma is on her cell phone, and when she stretches out her hand to take it back again, I slip it into a pocket and shake my head.

No sooner, however, than the phone disappears inside my jacket it rings. I shake my head again. "Selma Al-Khateeb is not available," I say. "Please leave your name and number and I'll return your call at my earliest convenience." But the possibility that this call will be NEWS is simply too much for her.

"It could be Mansour's lawyer," she says.

I remove the phone from my jacket and look at the screen. It is my wife. I wiggle my eyebrows in a vaguely salacious way and answer it myself. "You've reached the offices of Selma Al-Khateeb, World Traveler, currently stopping in Prague. How may I direct your call?"

"You are such a nerd," Stephanie says.

"Yes, but I'm a nerd who is out having fun while you are cooped up in a government office building slaving away for the man."

"Undeniable," she says. "In fact, I'm going to be stuck here longer than expected. Are you keeping Selma entertained?"

"We are on the street even now, being flaneurs."

"Wonderful. Listen, I've booked us on one of those boat tours later, so meet me at the dock at 7:30."

"Sounds good."

"Be nice to her."

"What else would I be?" I say and we hang up.

Selma is alternating between watching people on the street and smiling at my silly conversation. She seems happy, but tired and pained, the way your eyes hurt after you've done too much crying.

"We're on our own until 7:30," I say. "Let's get some of the basics out of the way."

"The basics?"

"Tourist trap number one: Old Town Square."

I walk her along the river where I had been on the night of Stephanie's birthday and let her get a good look at the castle and the bridge and the throngs of tourists milling about before meandering through the shops of the Staré Město to Old Town Square and the Old Town Hall with its famous astronomical clock. To really get the effect, I find us a table at one of the expensive restaurants on the square and order Pilsners and plates of appetizers. From here we'll have a perfect view of the clock. The dials and ephemera of the clock are beautiful, but the real fun starts when the hour strikes.

"Do you know about the clock?" I say.

"Just that it's famous."

"Or infamous. You'll soon discover that so many things in Prague are beautiful, but also dangerous and horrible."

And I tell Selma a little bit about the clock. How it was designed and built in the 15th century, that when the clock

strikes the hour the figure of Death pulls upon a rope, and miniature apostles, led by St. Peter, do a little mechanized lap, and
then a cock crows and the hour is chimed. It's a mechanized
puppet show, yes, but macabre. Another thing that Prague is
famous for.

We watch the clock perform its drama and Selma is delighted.
Of course there is so much else to look at: mimes and jugglers,
horse-drawn carriages that take riders around the square, little
troupes of Asian schoolgirls making each other's photographs.

"The authorities were so pleased with the clock that the man
who perfected it—his name was Hanuš—was blinded so that he
could never reproduce his work anywhere else in the world."

"That's horrible!"

"I told you. Beautiful and dangerous. Even the clock."

At the table beside us is a German couple who have been
drinking beer and taking photos of the square. The woman is
young and blonde and happy and keeps smiling at Selma and
me. As soon as I smile back, she asks us to take their photo.
Selma takes the camera from her, and the couple lean together
and put their arms around each other. "Say 'Prague'!" she says,
and when the Germans break into laughter, she snaps the picture.
Selma shows it to me and I nod my appreciation. A good shot.

"Thank you so much," the German woman says.

"Are you Americans?"

"Yes," I say.

"Do you enjoy Prague?"

I look at Selma to let her answer. "Oh yes, very much. It's so
beautiful, isn't it?"

"So beautiful!" the German woman says. "Is this your honeymoon?"

"What?" Selma says.

"You just look so happy together, I thought it must be your honeymoon," she says. "Dieter and I were married only last week."

"Congratulations!" Selma and I say together, and everybody laughs. Then I take Selma's hand and give it a squeeze. "No, this isn't our honeymoon. We've been married for ages."

I have no idea why I've said this other than in that moment I find there's a part of me that wishes it were true. I look at Selma to see how she'll react. For a moment her eyes become huge, but then she smiles and shakes her head the way that you would at a naughty but beloved child. "Oh, yes, ages," she says. "A hundred years."

"A thousand," I say, and again everyone laughs. Selma and I congratulate the Germans again and soon we are back to our own private conversations, except that for a little while neither Selma nor I seem to have anything to say to each other and so just watch the crowd and sip our drinks. The waiter breaks the spell of quietude when he arrives with our appetizers and I order us a second round of beer.

"Why is Prague so beautiful," Selma says, an oval of calamari pinned to her fork. "I don't remember the Czechs being famous for much other than being invaded by the Russians."

"Ugh, Selma. You're nothing but an unsophisticated American. I can't believe you just said that."

"I know. And Mansour's the same. Could you explain that to the FBI and INS? They don't seem to believe us."

"I'm sorry," I say.

"Oh, never mind. I'm feeling fine, really. Besides, now that you're my husband you're obligated to explain to me everything you've learned about Prague."

"Deal," I say. "Well, the reason the city is so beautiful, with the castle and the bridges, and the churches and everything, is that the Holy Roman Emperor Rudolph II moved his capital to Prague in the 16th century. Rudolph was a Catholic, but he wanted to create some separation between himself and the Vatican. I think he went to Vienna first but eventually settled here."

I explain to Selma that Rudolph was a collector of people and of things and that for a little while at least, Prague became the center of the world. Many people thought the emperor was crazy, but he was interested in everything. He brought in Europe's best writers and musicians and architects. He had an astounding library. He was also interested in magic and astrology. He paid for a whole army of alchemists that he had working on finding the Sorcerer's Stone and converting rocks into gold. They all lived up on the hill by the castle. I waved my arm in the general direction of the Vltava and the bridge.

"In fact, the Kafka house we're going to show you once housed some of Rudolph's alchemists."

"I'm trying to imagine it all," Selma said.

"With so much of the city intact you can almost do it—the buildings, the horse-drawn carriages. There are some streets that I could show you that no car could ever drive down. Of course, all the tourists don't help. Still, I love it here."

"You do love it, don't you?"

"I do. I don't ever want to go home."

"What if Stephanie gets reassigned?" Selma says.

"I don't let myself think about that." I smile.

Selma sits up a little straighter and takes a deep breath of the air. She looks up into the sun shining above the low buildings of the square and sighs. "Just between us, I don't want to go home either."

We go on in this way for a while, and I'm glad that Selma seems pleasantly distracted. It's not hard to do that here where so many things can go right. Yet I know that Stephanie will join us soon, and the little dynamic Selma and I have going will change. Perhaps for the better. Still, I will have to tell Stephanie later about Selma throwing her phone across the room, her frustration, how fragile she seems. And then the worrying will begin again. There will be plans and machinations, maybe even some kind of dramatic intervention, which I can see will be nothing but disastrous. I think of the expression on Selma's face when Stephanie was complaining about Margaret and Jeb, and I know that despite their shared past, something has slipped. Selma has changed.

———※———

The plan had been to walk and see as much of the city as we could until it was time to meet Stephanie, but each time I ask Selma if she is ready to move on she keeps saying, "Just a little while longer." And who could blame her. The later in the afternoon it becomes, the light changes so that it is softer and makes the stone of the old buildings glow. We watch this light and the people too, of course, and drink our Pilsners and become drunk. We say almost nothing to each other, but it's a good silence, the healthy kind, and somehow I'm not worried that Selma is thinking of Mansour or feeling guilty. She's just living. One sip of air at a time.

I look at my phone. Time for one more drink—at least.

When I signal the waiter I can feel Selma's eyes on me, watching. She has returned from her own private thoughts and is with me again. As she did yesterday, Selma piles her long hair on top of her head and holds it there for a moment to let the breeze cool the back of her neck. Then she lets it go and it falls down in waves onto her shoulders. I look at her and my look says, "You're beautiful," and Selma knows it.

"Thank you for bringing me here," Selma says. "For leaving work early and spending time with me."

"We'll thank Morgan later." I raise my beer and we clink our glasses together and take long drinks.

We sit there across from each other and everything seems fine, very fine in fact, but I have that feeling I did before Selma arrived, a kind of portent buzzing in the air between us. I think that she is working herself up to say something. No doubt all the beer has helped. I squeeze a little lemon onto what's left of the calamari and take a few bites and wait.

"You and Stephanie seem very happy," she says.

"We are, I think."

"You think?"

"I just mean that one never really knows, do they?" I say.

"Listen," she says, "I need you to do me a very big favor."

"What is it?" I say. "Anything."

"You better wait 'til you've heard what it is."

Selma is scrutinizing me. I can see her doing it, trying to decide something about me. Probably whether or not she can trust me. She looks for a long time at my face and hair, but her gaze takes in the details of my shirt and jacket and finally comes to rest on my hands, which are still holding the phone I used to check the time. I can't imagine what she thinks my body will tell her, but maybe she knows things that I cannot.

Well, what's your favor?

The fact that I can't even begin to imagine what it might be is the most disturbing part. I feel the same way I did when Michael called, unable to fathom how I could be in a position to help in any way, but game nonetheless.

"I need you to talk to Stephanie for me," she says.

"But you can talk to her yourself," I say. "She's your friend. She loves you."

"I know she does, but what I have to ask of her is difficult."

"Don't worry," I say. "We'd do anything we can for you."

"I want her to help me free Mansour."

Try to understand the naïveté that this request implies. Stephanie works in the United States Embassy in the Czech Republic. What possible connection can there be between the Foreign Service and the FBI? It's absurd. The bureaucracy of the government of the United States of America is so vast that my imagination can't even begin to account for it.

"We all want to help Mansour, but what can Stephanie do?"

Selma takes a swift, testy little breath, as though she's getting ready to embark on an explanation she's already made half a million times and I am a slightly dull pupil who she has no great confidence will understand no matter how careful she is.

"Of course I don't know exactly. But I feel certain that something can be done."

"Are the lawyers really making no progress at all?" I say. "You seemed very anxious about receiving a message today."

"Can I tell you the truth?"

"Yes," I say. "Absolutely."

"I think Mansour is going to die in that jail." She rakes her fingers into her hair just above each temple and holds them there for a moment. Frozen. "I know that sounds melodramatic to someone who's been so far away from these things, to someone whose life makes him safe from it."

Ouch. I pause for a moment to take it all in. That stings like hell; does not a Henry bleed? Am I incapable of feeling sadness or pain? I'd complain, but I think it's against the rules. And so I let it pass. Because I know she's in real pain. Because she's at the end of her rope.

Why does she seem so alone to me? Where are her parents? Her father was a minister in the Yemeni government and her mother worked for the World Bank. Surely they have resources that can be brought to bear. And what about Mansour? Don't I remember Stephanie telling me that his father was some kind of academic? They could at least be a support system for her, and yet I have not heard a single mention of them or of anything else that is actually being done on Mansour's behalf. Just this vague talk about lawyers.

"Well," I say to Selma, "if I can't possibly understand, then how is it that you think I could help?"

I think of what Stephanie had said to me in the limousine on the way to the Globe. *I want her to be surrounded by people who believe Mansour is innocent. Absolutely.*

"I will try very hard to explain things to you," Selma says. "Okay?"

The clock strikes the hour and we watch Death pull his rope and the apostles do their dance and the cock crow. Selma is irritated by the interruption and pulls painfully on the curl of hair lying against her temple so that she's almost pulling the skin away from her skull like Silly Putty.

Selma says, "I've done everything that I'm supposed to do. I've filled out every form, given them every document, hired a really, really good lawyer, started petitions, created a website to try to tell the world about Mansour's case and raise some money. And every month Mansour looks weaker and weaker. He was such a strong man, Henry, but now he's broken. This is going to kill him."

A loud, unexpected sob wells up from inside her and Selma covers her mouth with both hands. I can feel the German couple staring at us.

"There are things that can be done," I say. "I'm sure of it."

"I know. That's why you have to talk to Stephanie for me. There's a man who is handling Mansour's case. Jacob Sprecher. He went to law school at the University of Michigan in the mid-'90s. *Law Review.* There's a man in Stephanie's office who worked on Michigan's *Law Review* in 1996. Albert Jones.

They must know each other. I just need him to make a phone call. How simple is that? So easy. Nothing, really, in the big scheme of their lives. Just old friends catching up and talking about this coincidence that they have in common. Can you hear it, Henry, that easy conversation?" Selma puts her fingers up to her ear like a telephone receiver. "*'You won't guess who I have sitting across from me in our embassy in Prague. Mansour Al-Khateeb's wife.'* You see how simple it can be?"

This time Selma swallows the sob so that it comes out as a kind of strangled sound.

"Stephanie is a rule player," I say. "She won't want to do it that way." I try to make my voice as compassionate as possible.

"Don't you think I already know that?" Selma says. "That's why I need you to talk to her. I can't rely on the rules anymore—they don't apply to Arabs right now. I've followed them to the letter for the last fourteen months. I'm out of rules to follow. I just need a little help to get around the rules now, just a little opening. A foot in the door, you know? I swear if I had that I could do the rest."

"I believe you could," I say. I take a sip of my beer and look up at the sky. "So all that about wanting to see Kafka's house was bullshit?"

"No, it's not bullshit. Can't two things be true at once?"

"Promise me you won't say anything until I figure out how to approach her," I say.

"Not a word. Until you tell me otherwise."

Jesus fuck.

"Don't give up on other solutions, though. I want to think about those, too."

"Of course. Of course. I'm open to anything. Everything."

Selma reaches across our little table and takes my hand in both of hers. For a moment she simply holds them gently around mine but then bends down and begins to kiss my palm. One, two, three, four, five, six slow, lingering kisses, her lips moist, her soft hair tickling my skin.

When Selma raises her head again, she's smiling. It's a kind smile. A little sad, maybe.

"You're the best kind of man. I'm so grateful."

"It's going to be all right," I say, but I'm still thinking of the way her lips felt on me and she knows it. I can still feel their lingering presence even now. She raises her beer to her lips and drinks the rest of it down quick, and I do the same. It's funny to watch this frail Arab woman matching me drink for drink with the big stein in front of her face. There's a moment when both our drinks are tipped back and our synchronized movements make us smile. Finally I pay our bill and we leave.

When we get away from the tangle of tables and chairs and into the open square, Selma takes my arm and leans her head against my shoulder as we walk. I don't want to make love to Selma just now, but I am transported—there's no other word for it—by this intimacy with a woman who is not my wife. I have loved Stephanie so much, with all of myself, and for so long, that I had cut off all ideas of this kind of feeling for another woman. To know someone else and to be known by her. The thrill of the possibility of discovering another human being is, along with the Pilsner, intoxicating. I wonder if Selma feels it too.

But I am forgetting Mansour, and Selma, surely, is not.

So okay, for a moment I let myself play with the idea of being a tragic hero. Don Quixote perhaps, or Humphrey Bogart's character in *Casablanca*, or best of all, Cyrano de Bergerac—martyring himself to the unworthy rival who is elevated to sainthood by his death in battle. Yes, Cyrano then. Imagine the long, flowing cloak, the rapier at his side, the imposing mustaches, the rare wit.

She whispers my name as we walk. "Henry." By which she means, thank you. "It's going to be all right," I say again.

"I know."

"You'll see."

Selma is leaning so close to me that I can feel the subtle rolling of her hips as she walks. The exquisite shifting of weight from hip to hip, even in a woman as slight as Selma. I think to gently push away from her, to stop and point out some Czech architectural triumph, but the tension is too exquisite.

Hate yourself, Henry, I think. *You are being unfaithful in your heart.* But I can't take myself seriously. Everything feels too good.

Save yourself. Go find Stephanie. Now.

———————

Flaneurs again, but no longer alone. Stephanie is able to leave the embassy earlier than she thought and joins us for some shopping in the Staré Město. In a shop selling exquisite Czech crystal, my wife sneaks up behind me and puts her hands over my eyes. Nips at my ear.

"Guess who?"

"Paulina Porizkova."

"No, asshole, it's your wife."

"One of these times," I say, "it's going to be Paulina."

"You wish. Where's Selma?"

Selma is talking to the shop girl, a tall supermodel from Kazakhstan who became incredibly excited when she learned that Selma has lived in New York. It's almost nice that someone in the world still gets excited about New York. I, of course, can't imagine wanting to be anywhere other than Prague.

Stephanie joins her friend at the counter and I watch them embrace, kissing each other on the cheek and smiling.

"What are you buying?" Stephanie says.

"These wineglasses. They say they'll ship them home for me."

I wait to see if Stephanie stops her from buying the crystal here. There are other places and cheaper, but to my surprise she says nothing about it, just gushes over how beautiful the glasses are. Whatever makes Selma happy, that's the ticket.

Would Stephanie think so if she knew how I'd spent the afternoon, beating off thinking about her friend and then machinating with that friend to manipulate her?

There is so much to tell Stephanie that I almost don't know where to begin. Somehow, though, I'll need to tell her just how desperate Selma has become.

"I'm going to just walk around a bit on my own," I tell Stephanie quietly. "Give you guys some time alone together."

"You're sweet," she says and kisses me. "I'll call you when it's time to meet our ship."

I step out of the shop and into the deep throng of tourists.

The sun has softened almost entirely now and what I think of as a European coolness has descended on the streets as the city prepares for evening. The side streets that lead away from Old Town Square are meandering cobblestone paths, densely packed with tiny shops: Czech Republic memorabilia, expensive wooden puppets, handmade jewelry, pashmina scarves, art galleries. The entire neighborhood has become a riotous capitalist cancer. Or cure.

I turn down Karlova, then to Anenska and the river. I don't know where I'm going exactly, just away from the worst of the crowds where I can do a little thinking. I can see the National Theatre in the not-too-far distance and decide to make for it. The traffic flies by on the Masarykovo nábřeží, which makes for a different kind of distraction than the tourists, a new kind of aloneness. The wind blows my hair and jacket. I can smell the water off to the right and occasionally look back to get a glimpse of the castle and the bridge—they pull the gaze like a magnet. The cars that pass by are almost all German and expensive, with a smattering of Škodas and Peugeots. All of these wealthy people to-ing and fro-ing around Prague, vacationing for a few days before returning to Munich or Vienna or Budapest. What are they preparing to do this evening? Go out to dinner, take in a performance at the National Theatre that most Praguers can't afford? Perhaps something slightly less pedestrian? An evening spent in the company of a beautiful Czech prostitute, a thing that is more difficult to do now than it was ten years ago but still easy enough, especially if you don't mind Roma? They are not necessarily the most vulgar picture snappers, but they are maybe a little self-satisfied with their disposable incomes and slightly too exuberant sophistication. I shouldn't complain, though, should I? They are my best customers. A book purchased at the Hades isn't just a book, it's a story to be told over a sherry back in Lyon or Madrid, a story of the little English-language bookshop with its clever name. Truly, I couldn't do without them—and neither could Prague.

However, if I were to veer south and farther away from the center of the city, it's the Czechs who would be looking at me with their inscrutable eyes that do not quite hide their contempt for the way Prague has been overrun with foreigners.

Better think about something else. And then it strikes me: Anthony.

His visit to the shop this afternoon was a mystery, and I had almost forgotten about it with all that's been on my mind since then. What is he up to, wanting to meet Selma? To help show her a good time, to show off his *New York Times* lover, to be part of things? Maybe. But the Anthony I know would want to lay in a couple of bottles of vodka, lock the door to his apartment, and fuck that woman senseless for as long as she'd let him. I trust him, I do, really. That doesn't change the fact that I didn't like the way he wouldn't look me in the eye when he suggested his little outing with Selma. Something's not right and that worries me. Still—and this is what has struck me—there might be more than one way to shed the light of day on Mansour's case.

I stop walking and lean against the front window of the Café Slavia. Then I scroll down the contacts in my phone until I find Anthony's name and press Send.

He'll answer if he's not working, sometimes even if he is. Anthony lives faithfully with his cell phone in a way that he never has with a woman.

"Hey, Henry, you prick. I was just thinking about you."

"Sure you were," I say. "What's news?"

This is our normal pre-conversation banter. Absolutely adolescent, a thing that no amount of money or education seems to be able to beat out of us.

"I'm at the Senate getting ready to file a story. Pretty hot debate on the missile systems."

"You're an important man. I've always said it."

Now that it's come to asking for my own favor, I feel inexplicably nervous, like some kind of charlatan who will be too easily unmasked. It's absurd. I've been shit-faced with this man, walking arm in arm through Wenceslas Square singing '80s pop songs. INXS suddenly leaps to mind.

"What are you up to?" Anthony says.

"Shopping with Stephanie and Selma."

I think I can picture Anthony perfectly: standing in one of the little courtyards outside the Senate building, perhaps leaning against a column. There's almost no security there, and I've often thought that some crank could just walk in and start shooting. Yet in twenty years no one has. I can hear a sharp intake of breath on the line and know that Anthony is smoking. Benson & Hedges, if I remember correctly. He still hasn't given it up, yet another of those journalistic prerogatives. And although it's been almost five years since my last cigarette, I feel a pang of nicotine nostalgia.

"Actually, I'm walking on my own right now," I say. "Giving the ladies a little space. That kind of thing."

"You sound like you've been drinking most of the afternoon."

"Maybe."

"Lucky bastard," Anthony says. "Beautiful day, beautiful women, beautiful Pilsners. And I've been stuck inside listening to a lot of old farts discuss the fate of the country."

"Well," I say. "They pay you."

"Goddamn right."

A woman and her son have taken the table just on the other side of the window inside the Café Slavia. She's wearing a cream-colored Chanel dress, the kind of thing that Princess Diana might have worn ten years ago. Her son looks like a little gentleman. I give them both a quick smile before pushing away from the window and crossing the street to sit on a bench in front of the National Theatre.

"Listen," I say. "I wanted to talk to you about earlier today."

I can almost smell the gears working in Anthony's mind as he tries to anticipate my angle. I don't think he can help it. This is what he does.

"Sounds serious," he says. "Is everything okay?"

"It might be serious. That's why I'm calling you."

Down the block two Roma are shouting jovially to tourists, asking people to buy them beers. They are probably harmless, but they look rough, unwashed with long, twisting mustaches.

They are shirtless but wear the vests from old suits, which have a kind of sinister effect. I think to move on, away from the theater so they don't come by to hassle me, but I don't. I just stay put and gawk at them like everyone else.

"Henry, you still there?"

"What? Yes. There's just some people on the street."

"Imagine," he says. "People on the street in Prague in June."

Quite suddenly I just want to hang up. Walk away into the evening as if I'd not talked to Selma this afternoon or dialed Anthony's number now. I think of a little inside joke between Stephanie and me, a thing she says on those rare occasions when life seems just too much for her and she doesn't, under any circumstances, want to set foot anywhere near the embassy, just a little quote from Melville's Bartleby, "I would prefer not to." And so it is with me this moment. A dropped call, I could tell him later. Such things happen. I would prefer not to. Yet again, though, I don't do anything, say anything.

"Henry?"

"Yes, I know, I know. I'm here."

"Time is money, old man," Anthony says, but he doesn't mean it. He's only teasing me so I'll know it's okay to say whatever it is I have to tell him.

"Something is wrong," he adds.

"Well, this afternoon you were suggesting that we all go out with Selma."

"Yes, to U Sudu."

"You wanted to bring your *New York Times* friend, right?"

"Yeah, Belinda. Wonderful girl."

"Belinda. Right. Listen, I think that might be a good idea."

Anthony doesn't say anything right away, and I know he's trying to figure out why this should have been so difficult for me to say. Again I am choked with the desire to run away. But then I remember the feel of Selma's lips on my hand.

"I'm glad you think it's a good idea," he finally says. "No doubt that's why I had it."

"Look, Anthony, I'm sorry. I'm not making myself very clear."

"No, old man, you're really not. How drunk are you?"

Not nearly drunk enough, though I don't say this.

"Look," I say, "here's what it boils down to. I know you've got some kind of angle or you wouldn't be sharing Belinda with the rest of the world. I just can't figure what it is. As it turns out, I've got something of an angle, too. Let's make an agreement: You tell me yours and I'll tell you mine, and no harm done either way."

"Jesus," Anthony says, "what were they serving you this afternoon? The paranoid Pilsners?"

"Something like that. But all bullshit aside, why does Belinda want to meet Selma?"

"Fuck, you are a cagey little motherfucker, aren't you?"

"Not especially. I've just known you for a long time."

"All right. So here's how it went down. At Stephanie's party I'm talking to Michael and he spills the beans about Selma coming to town and the whole thing with her husband."

"Go on."

"So then Belinda blows into town and she's just done this piece on the domestic consequences of the War on Terror and

I say, 'Shit, baby. You'll never guess but even the domestic is global,' and so to impress her I tell her all about Selma."

"Kind of like, sure you write for the *Times*, but don't think Prague is some backwater."

"Right. I'm trying to get laid over here," he says.

"I thought she was a sure thing?"

"She is, but every little bit helps."

Though I don't really mean to, I am assaulted with pornographic images of Anthony engaged with a gartered Belinda. It's hot as hell in his apartment and both of them are sweating vodka while looking out of his third-story window at the view of Prague. Probably I'm imagining a much better sex life for my friend than is actually true. Regardless, what I really want now is that cigarette, but I know it's my turn to come clean.

"How much do you trust this Belinda?" I say.

"Look, I don't know what's up, but you don't become a regular for the *Times* by screwing your sources. I wouldn't give the girl a thousand dollars and the keys to my car, but she's a good reporter."

"Fair enough. Okay. Let's just say that Selma might actually want to talk to Belinda. Her husband—his name's Mansour—is really up against it. They've been holding him for fourteen months without a charge."

"They can do that."

"I know. And Selma thinks she's exhausted all of her options. Turns out she came to Prague almost entirely to convince Stephanie to use some supposed government connection to get him freed."

"What's Stephanie think of that?"

"We haven't told her yet."

"*We?*"

"Yeah," I say.

"Be careful, man. This isn't your kind of thing," he says. "This isn't Anna-fucking-Karenina. This is the real thing."

"That's why I'm calling you."

I say this to Anthony, but I'm not sure I entirely mean it. The journalist has one morality: expose, expose, expose. Drag life out into the light of day and let readers pass judgment. It's a noble enterprise. The Fourth Estate and all that. But too often that single-mindedness can be traced back to the egos of individual journalists or even newspapers—if institutions can have egos. Sometimes a little bit more subtlety is called for.

"Look, I know it seems like Selma's got her head on her shoulders. Manipulating me, manipulating Stephanie, but that's not the whole story. This woman is in a bad way, really. I've just spent the last day and a half with her and she's ready to break. Whatever happens later, whatever you and your friend dream up, we've got to be careful with her."

"We will, we will."

"No. She has to be a person first and a story second. Anything fucked up happens, you've got to be prepared to walk away."

Anthony doesn't say anything, and I don't either. Give him time to think. I look out at the stream of cars on Masarykovo nábřeží and lose myself for a moment in their speed and movement. I think of my own car, garaged quietly for the last two weeks. More escape fantasies.

"Are you still there?" I say.

"Yeah, I'm still here."

His voice sounds deflated, a hopped-up teenager chafing at the constraint on his enthusiasm. Neither of us can guarantee the other's behavior, so he might as well just agree.

"Okay," he says. "I'll dig out a couple pairs of kid gloves."

"Thanks, Anthony."

Across the street the Slavia is gearing up for dinner as though someone opened a floodgate. Stephanie will doubtless call any minute. Then on to the riverboat, some half-baked buffet and an hour of sightseeing. At least, I think, the liquor on board will be wet. I tell Anthony the details of our plans.

"We'll call you when we've docked," I say.

"'Til then," Anthony says, and he is gone.

Seven

I am wrecked: The mouth it is dry, the head it pounds. Somewhere, deep beneath the engorged fur of my tongue there is the faint aftertaste of shrimp. I am nearly blind. A horrifying cocktail of Pilsner and Johnnie Walker Red sputtering and smoking in my stomach like the fires of Mt. Etna. Without thinking I stagger into the living room, wearing only a pair of light blue boxers decorated with a pattern of Jack Russell terriers, where I hear Stephanie preparing herself for the embassy.

In the kitchen my wife is making coffee. "Nice underwear," she says to me, squinting without contacts or glasses. "I'm sure Selma's sorry she's missing them."

"Huh?" I say. I look down at the dogs. "Oh right, Selma." For about three blessed minutes, I have actually forgotten about our guest. "Remind me," Stephanie says, "to never let you talk me into drinking with journalists ever again."

"It's entirely possible a crime was committed last night."

Stephanie snorts but says nothing more. For a few minutes we just stand there, hung over together, inhaling the divine scent of brewing coffee. How many times have we found ourselves like this after what Stephanie calls a "room-spinning drunk"? So many, and yet not so many recently. It brings us back a little, I can see it on the amused half smile that cracks through the mask of her own morning-after symptoms.

"Last night was an interesting meeting of the minds," I say when she hands me a steaming cup of black coffee.

"It certainly was. Whose idea was that?"

"Anthony's, if you can believe it," I say. "Oh God, that's good coffee."

"Really? How did he even know Selma was in town?"

"Michael."

"Of course."

"He came to see me at the Hades. The moment I understood that he was voluntarily limiting his pillow time with Belinda I knew something was up."

"That man will do anything to get laid."

I raise an eyebrow and nod in agreement. For a little while

we stand there together and drink our coffee, but I can see that Stephanie's mind is at work. She does this little thing with her lower lip, sawing her front teeth back and forth across the chapped flesh. Sometimes her efforts are so vigorous that she has to stop and pick away little flakes of skin. It's an endearing move, something that she will do only when she is alone or with me. I take it as one of those many little signs that pass for love in a long marriage such as ours.

"You could say their meeting was mutually beneficial, right?"

"It could work that way," she says. "Belinda will win regardless."

"I suppose so."

"And Anthony probably won early this morning." Again, between sips of coffee Stephanie gives her almost-smile.

She takes down the aspirin from the kitchen cabinet and then swallows two extra-strength capsules before throwing the bottle to me.

"Even if the story Belinda writes only causes a momentary buzz," Stephanie says and then lowers her voice to a whisper, "Selma will feel like she did something."

"Yes," I say, but my tone isn't especially convincing.

"You don't think that's good enough?"

This is Stephanie hitting me where I live. All my adult life I have been an advocate of the gesture; my hero Cyrano would certainly approve (*the best fight is the one you know is in vain*), and my wife knows this. To do a good thing, to follow an action that has integrity to its conclusion regardless of its effectiveness, has been something I've tried to live by.

To say bluntly that making such a gesture is not good enough would be to contradict myself. But now I find myself thinking not of Cyrano but of Lytton Strachey and of Bloomsbury. No doubt this is because of Thien Diep and her *Lighthouse*, and I am impressed by the way the mind can ping-pong its way from scrap of influence to scrap of influence without really missing a beat. Strachey was a conscientious objector and had to defend himself both in writing and in court to avoid military service in WWI. Strachey was probably not fit for service regardless, but the idea that an individual could make an appeal to his government and have it heard and acted upon makes me have confidence in people. I imagine Virginia Woolf and Vanessa Bell and Dora Carrington and all the rest of the Bloomsbury crew sitting on the benches behind Strachey as he makes arguments for his freedom. All those talented young women lending their strength and charisma to the cause. My romantic heart hopes that this may be what Belinda's article represents for Selma and Mansour. But I fear it will only be a gesture.

"What more can be done?" she says when I don't answer.

Perhaps something else. Just do it, I think. Just tell her. It's your wife, for God's sake. And still I keep it back.

"I don't know," I say. "I wish I did."

"It's nice to see you care. I wasn't sure you really did."

"Oh, thanks."

"Well, that is how it seemed."

I open the aspirin bottle and take two of my own. I become very interested in my coffee and then stroll over to the window for a look down to the street. I feel suddenly exposed and have this irrational concern that Selma will come out from her bed to see me like this, half naked and completely hungover.

"Isn't there something going on at the embassy today?"

Of course I already know that the Assistant Secretary of State is flying in to lend weight to the missile defense negotiations. It's a bad habit of mine, asking questions that I already know the answer to. Still, my memory often gives the impression that I care about the details of Stephanie's working life—a thing that rarely fails to score me points.

"Indeed. The Assistant Secretary is coming."

Stephanie's job is an important one. She will be the one who mediates the different personalities because she is the one, after all, who actually knows the Czechs, knows the names of their wives and children, who understands the finer points of Central European etiquette, which can be just as important as carrying presidential authority.

I know from long experience that it is for moments like these that Stephanie went to work for the government, these moments where it's possible to actually have an influence.

I don't envy her in the slightest.

"It is kind of exciting," she says, and for the first time the liquor-induced sluggishness with which she has greeted the day is thrown off. Her eyes grow brighter and, I swear, her skin tauter and more youthful-looking.

"You're going to be great," I say, comfortable in my role as cheerleader to greatness. "Kick ass, take names."

"You're such a nerd. You don't even have an opinion about the missile system."

"Guilty," I say.

She offers me more coffee and I accept. For a moment as she's pouring the steaming liquid into my cup we are standing very close. I can smell the rich odor of her that sleep has collected and take the opportunity to kiss her on the cheek. *Tell her about Selma's favor. Go on. All will be well.*

"Did I tell you I'm going out to Kutna Hora today?"

"To see Thien Diep?"

I nod. "She wants to sell a perfectly good *To the Lighthouse*."

"Well then help her. And charge her a whole lot of money to do it."

"Ye-es," I say.

I have to admit that Stephanie's pretty good at keeping up with the details, too. I've talked about Thien Diep enough times and we've certainly made money from her business, but it's still impressive—considering all the truly important things that might be on my wife's mind at any given time—that she can find space there for my day-to-day as well. Stephanie loves the idea of what I do, this literary life she thinks is a nice thing to swim along beside, and she likes the parties, the people, the books. She also likes the way that the relative balance of power in our relationship tilts to her. Career diplomat or bookstore owner? No contest, really. Yet she seems to understand that this life creates for me both drama and fulfillment, even if it would eventually leave her cold should our roles be reversed. She would have been quietly amused by the enthusiasm that Morgan and I showed over the Borges manuscript. She would not have felt the need to touch the pages, would not have felt any sense of reverence over reading the Master's handwriting, to sharing an experience that has survived for decades its journey though a dangerous world.

"She's almost certainly going to sell it at a loss," I say, "though I guess it should all be the same to me."

And it is certainly all the same to Stephanie, who is rightly preoccupied with the Assistant Secretary of State and Selma Al-Khateeb.

"Well, Thien's an odd woman," she says, and there's a finality to this comment as Stephanie empties the dregs of her coffee into the sink and stretches, her arms extending high above her head. She's about to turn toward the bathroom for a shower, and this might be my last chance to say anything of note to my wife for the rest of the day and maybe longer.

"I need your advice," I say.

"About what?"

"You don't think it was a mistake to put Selma and Anthony together?"

"No, I don't," she says. "But even if it was, Selma's a big girl. She can handle herself."

Normally, I think, Stephanie would be right. But this is a new Selma. "You're sweet," Stephanie says and kisses me.

When we've both showered and dressed, I leave her making phone calls on her BlackBerry and waiting for a car to pick her up for the airport where they will meet the Assistant Secretary. She is dressed in an expensive charcoal-gray suit and skirt, long hair curling onto her shoulders the only thing breaking up the career-woman mystique. I wish suddenly that I were such a man who would have such a woman coming to meet him at the airport.

"Once more unto the breach," I say. "Call me if anything exciting happens."

"I will."

When Stephanie's attention returns to her phone, I take a quick glance at the door behind which Selma is lying on our pullout bed, her hair spilled out across the pillow, before heading out into the Prague morning.

My train doesn't leave until 10:25, and so I stop in to visit Morgan at the Hades. Or rather, I stop in to visit the known world, my world, with its books and wood and the scent of dust and paper. It's a good idea, too, a moment to reorient the mind to business, which Thien Diep will require. Morgan looks to be in his own quiet mode after a sleepless night or drinking binge or who knows what, and I can see that while I might be able to tell him about Selma—about what I've already done and, worse, what I'm afraid I might soon do—he's in no place to offer any advice. And besides, I'm afraid of a kind of catty impatience with which he might greet my hopelessly heterosexual problems. He's probably also a bit envious that my working day will consist of a pleasant train ride after which I will visit a beautiful house to talk about books and be given a drink, maybe even a late lunch.

Even so, it would be nice to not feel so out to sea, to get a little advice. Michael might be the most likely candidate for such a conversation. There would be no judgment delivered, just a cool, masculine analysis of the situation. But for the moment, Selma is my secret and one I think might be best kept to myself. Oddly, I don't want to give Michael anything on me. That feels false, Machiavellian, and probably paranoid, but that's how it is. I remember Stephanie's advice, that Michael rarely does anything without seeing his own advantage. So, no Michael. Suddenly I am looking forward to a train that will take me out of the city.

The trains that travel to Vienna or Munich or Budapest are very much like trains anywhere in the EU—cushioned, air-conditioned, coffee service—but the trains that provide domestic service within the Czech Republic are another matter altogether. They are heavy iron monstrosities from another time, clanking and shifting on the tracks so that passengers feel every bump and sway. And it is one of the surest ways to find yourself surrounded almost entirely by Czechs speaking in their own language and eating long ham sandwiches brought from home. Children hang out the windows laughing and waving to strangers and no one yells at them to stop. Even without a necktie I am clearly the odd man out in my gray suit and briefcase. The adults fuel their analysis of me with quick, furtive glances while the children simply stare openly with their large, otherworldly eyes. It isn't at all unpleasant, though it is warm, while the train makes its slow way through the Prague suburbs. Before long I have to stand and remove my jacket, roll up the cuffs of my shirtsleeves.

It's a fairly pleasant trip, and brief, the whole experience over in less than two hours. I can't read with all the swaying, but I'm content to look out the window at the Czech villages, their small white houses with red-tiled roofs. An old woman in a flower-print dress carries a basket into a little church. I can't stop myself from indulging in rural fantasies of village life. How quiet it might be. How human the scale. The train stops occasionally at little stations to pick up a handful of passengers. I am in love with the sensation of shuttling out of the city and into something else entirely.

Kutna Hora when we arrive does not immediately have this kind of charm. The station is quaint and sheltered from the world by a long tree-lined fence, but beyond this barrier something much less picturesque awaits. It's actually a good-sized town, but without enough revenue to unmake fifty years of Soviet influence. Certain sections have the look of broken-down suburbs dominated by the ubiquitous cement-block apartment buildings. In Prague where these structures exist, residents have started to paint their buildings in pastel colors to liven things up, but not here. In these parts of Kutna Hora the only thing that breaks up the monotony are the potted flowers on the tiny balconies.

But Kutna Hora is an old town, too. There is the Bone Church, of course, that I will avoid today. There is the town center that possesses much of Prague's Old Town charm. There is the St. Barbara's Church, which is an absolute Gothic wonder and, beyond the cathedral, high up on the hill, is Thien Diep's home.

Thien used to drive down to the station to pick me up on my visits, but I finally convinced her that I like the walk. If you go slowly, as I often do, it can take forty minutes. But I don't mind.

Once I'm past those old Soviet outskirts and into the town itself, there are courtyards hiding tiny beer halls and restaurants, ice cream shops, even a bookstore. Four months ago, on my last visit, I was walking through the town, rounded a cobblestone corner and nearly ran into the most beautiful woman I have ever seen. She was a girl, really, a teenager. Fifteen years old, perhaps. She was out walking with her friend looking for something to do. They had that look about them, bored, a little indolent. She was tall and lithe, long dark hair and, though it pains me to talk about anyone like this, eyes like sapphires. We exchanged a long look as we passed each other and something fundamental, like gravity, shifted in my stomach. The expression in those eyes felt ancient and a little haunting, and we both turned around twice to keep looking at each other until a corner was turned and she was gone. Spooky. Sometimes I find myself staring off into the distance and I see her face, those eyes, and wonder what she had been thinking. That I was foreign, no doubt, that I had a life that was bigger than hers. As I walk today, I find that I can't help looking for her.

To shake off thoughts of this girl, I do what has always come most naturally: I think about books.

Because of Thien, I know Kutna Hora better than any other place in the Czech Republic outside of Prague. And I wonder, as I always have, what Thien is doing here. This little provincial town, this macabre tourist trap? Great literature has always needed its patrons, its salon makers, someone to adore the possible and to pour the wine. Traditionally this kind of thing has taken place in cities: Paris, most famously, London, New York.

Prague in the '90s, and before I arrived, was heralded as the new Paris. It was romantic and beautiful and cheap. And yet very little has come of it. Prague could use a Thien Diep with her eccentricities, her niece playing the piano, her undeniable taste and deep pockets. Instead, we have Kutna Hora—sometimes beautiful, yes—but a place where the most interesting people in town are already dead and teenagers specialize in escape fantasies.

But perhaps Thien understands something that I do not.

Sooner than I am ready, I find myself walking the long, crushed-stone drive that leads to Thien's home. It is a big place, though not immense, not an *estate*—a house. She had the place built to fit in with the local aesthetic: white walls, red roof tiles that already look as though they've existed for a century. There is a little fountain out front, a cupid peeing voraciously, and a wide turnaround drive. Under the shade of a portico I take a moment's cool relief from the sun before ringing the bell.

Almost immediately I hear a bustle and then a clicking of heels on the tiled floor and Thien herself answering her own door.

"Henry!" she shouts, a ball of energy and excitement. "You've made it!"

"*C'est moi, c'est moi, madame,*" I say and we both laugh at our little faux cultural moment.

Inside the entry hall is an amusing amalgamation of East and West with two framed paintings by Bloomsbury artists—one a Carrington, one a Duncan Grant hanging above thin-legged tables that are covered with Buddhist statuettes and a Czech crystal vase filled with orange lilies.

I want to stop and admire the paintings more closely, but Thien is always hurrying me along. The house smells of flowers and sunshine and its owner's perfume. Thien's personality is so vital, I am pulled along in its wake. Try not to think about how I seem always to be in thrall to the whims of one woman or another and what that might say about me. Just follow along like a good boy, be charming, see if she's offering an old book for me to sell.

When we enter her library, I find that I'm suddenly aware of my breathing, panting, almost dog-like as if I needed immediately to cool something down. Before I actually go in, I pause and take a deep breath. Fix a smile on my face. It is in place just when Thien realizes that I have not followed her.

Thien smiles, too, mistaking my hesitation for reverence. The Diep collection. Almost fourteen hundred books. Three hundred Bloomsburys and the rest rare editions of early-20th-century British and British Colonial literature. I could name nearly every book by heart, having helped Thien create and update a catalogue for each of the last three years. This room, I think, is the center of Thien's life. A source of immense satisfaction and pleasure, and feelings that I get to participate in by association. I shake off a little shiver of envy for Thien's disposable income.

The library is a long, narrow room flooded with natural light from two windows that run nearly floor to ceiling. Sculpted shrubbery just outside seems to frame the glass with green and casts wonderful geometric shadows onto the floor and along the gleaming surface of a baby grand. An intricate Czech crystal chandelier descends into the center of the room, which is neatly crowded with couches and club chairs and bookcases and long wooden tables artfully stacked with recent acquisitions waiting to be shelved. And there, of course, is Thien herself standing now in the center of it all with her wide, infectious smile, her hands held palms up above her head, as if to say *"Ta-da,"* her obvious pride nearly crackling through her skin. Every collector that I have ever met is enthusiastic, almost to the point of obsession, but most like to play it cool—at least for as long as self-control allows. But not Thien. It seems that she can't be bothered to construct a pose. She has money and she likes to spend it on the things she loves, and she doesn't care who knows it or what judgment they might deliver.

Thien Diep.

She's not quite an original, but she is rare and eccentric. Short and pale, a woman who was probably thin as a girl and a young married woman, but who has thickened a little now in her late fifties. Her dark hair is dyed jet black and spiked straight up with a thick gel so that pods of hair are twisted together like the bristles of an old hairbrush. Today she wears slacks the color of stone and a long navy blouse woven through with silver flowers.

"Is all as you remember it, Henry?" she says. Her voice is playful, confident that I will fall in love with this room, with these books, with her, all over again.

"Even more wonderful than I remember it."

Thien places both palms to her lips and then extends her hands to me blowing a kiss, her fingers wiggling to help it make its way across the room. She seems to love these theatrics and to appreciate my role as the eternal straight man in our routine.

"I know I act like a tyrant on the phone, but I really am grateful that you're willing to travel so far," she says. This, too, is all part of the game. She has gotten what she wanted and can afford to be polite, to give a little here, now, in exchange for what she hopes to get.

"It's no trouble at all."

Thien sits down on the couch and pats the cushion beside her for me to follow.

"As I told you yesterday, I want to sell my *Lighthouse*. It's not a bad copy at all. In fact, I've been very happy with it in so many ways, but . . . I don't know quite how to put it. It's lost its luster."

I can't agree, of course, but I'm determined not bring up any opposition to Thien's plan. It would be useless in any case.

"Well, I'm sure we can find a buyer for you," I say. "That's no trouble. But more importantly, as I've said, I'm off very soon to look at a substantial new collection in Brno. The man's name is Milos Nemec."

"Yes, you said. Someone related to Michael."

"To Michael's wife, Anna. Her uncle."

"He's a collector?"

I can see Thien trying to place Nemec among people she knows or at least may have heard of by reputation. Serious collectors pride themselves on knowing one another, on being insiders. That there should be someone with a major collection so close, and yet unknown, is probably vexing to her.

"Not exactly. It's a long-standing family collection most recently cared for by his wife. She died some years back."

"And now he's fallen on hard times through drink or gambling and needs to sell it all off?"

"Something of that order. A bad natural gas investment. But yes, it's the old story all over again."

I decide to keep the details of Michael and Anna's connection to the investment to myself. Thien's a wonderful woman in many ways, but she's a gossip, and it wouldn't be long before rumors of Michael's financial demise came trickling back to the city. And, of course, Michael would have no trouble tracing its source to me.

"You think he'll have something for me?"

"I haven't seen even a single book yet, so I can't say for sure. But Michael says it's a large English-language collection. I like our chances."

"Oh, that is too exciting. I almost wish I could come with you," she says.

"I know. I have to admit, I'm pretty damn excited myself."

The whole time we are talking my attention is slightly distracted by a glass-topped case just behind the couch where we're sitting. The glass top lifts like a lid on brass hinges and inside there is a bed of shimmering blue velvet. The interior of the case can be softly lit by two bulbs that are snugly fit into the sides. I know from my past visits that four books are carefully arranged on the velvet, all Bloomsbury, all Hogarth Press—the pride of Thien's collection. The whole room, but especially this case, gives off a warm, dusty smell that is like an aphrodisiac for the book lover. And the case itself tickles some deep sense memory of regional museums, far off the beaten path, filled with faded photographs or spent bullets or crumbling letters with cramped and antiquated handwriting.

Not able to wait any longer, I get up and stand over the case. The book in question: Virginia Woolf's *To the Lighthouse*. I already know all of its particulars. Hogarth Press, 1927. A first edition. Its condition is very good in a very good dust cover with some chipping at the spine and corners, some little tanning of the spine. The original paper of the jacket has been archivally strengthened at the folds, else the jacket is entirely original and has no supplemental restoration—very rare. Octavo. The original bright blue cloth, 320 pages. I can remember, word for word, the description that I wrote of the novel before Thien acquired it: One of the author's most influential novels, a richly textured examination of gender and family, told through stream-of-consciousness narratives. A nice, unsophisticated copy of a masterwork of modern literature. Thien purchased the book for $18,500.

In my estimation it is worth every penny. First, it is rare. One of only three thousand copies. I don't want to be too romantic about it, but just imagine who might have been among the first readers of those books, perhaps this very copy. John Maynard Keynes? E.M. Forster? T.S. Eliot? And Hogarth being such a small operation, I like to pretend that each book was handled by Leonard Woolf himself and, quite possibly, by Virginia. It is not at all such a far-flung idea. And the dust jacket designed by Virginia's sister, Vanessa Bell. I have always thought that the image was a kind of phantasmagoric tree hemmed in by a black scalloped border, but that makes little sense. Much more likely it is, of course, a lighthouse with a burst of light at the top that I have always mistaken for leaves, the blue and black swirls at the bottom, ocean waves crashing onto the beach. It is those thick lines of blue that I love the best, the way they leap out at the viewer. The colors are muted, but the design is so utterly recognizable as Bell, a style that gave so many of the Hogarth Press books their distinctive look. The book is light in the hand yet substantial, too. I don't know how else to say it except that it feels *right*, as it should, though I could not even begin to describe what I mean. I wonder, not for the first time, if Thien has read it. I don't mean Woolf's novel in general, but this copy in particular. It's a thing that many dealers don't like to talk about, a kind of unspoken shame to us that many of the clients who purchase these most expensive of books rarely read them. They are collectors of rare artifacts, concerned primarily with their value, with making sure that no further foxing or chipping should occur, that no oil from a reader's fingertips should degrade the pages. And this *is* a way to own books. And I am not really complaining, because collectors like that keep my little world spinning. Still, I think, a book like this *Lighthouse* is meant to be read. I can't bring myself to ask Thien if she has or not.

In fact, though, this book is no longer just a book. It is an artifact of a certain time, a particular moment. It holds within its paper and binding not just the inky symbols of Woolf's text but an idea of the world, of life, that is going away or that is already gone. A family is at the beach, yes, and guests arrive at their house, yes, and there is some discussion of whether or not an excursion will be made to the lighthouse, yes. But these things can be derived from any new paperback copy. But open this particular book, 1927, first edition, and carefully place your nose between the pages and you can breathe in the very air of the past. A time machine, lying there under the glass of Thien's case.

"May I?" Thien nods her consent.

Carefully, I open the case and let the scent of the books fill my nose like the bouquet from a freshly poured glass of cabernet. I pick up the book gently with both hands and remember its weight. I examine in detail the foxing and chipping, the slight discolorations that less careful owners have perpetrated upon this rare object. Then I open the text to the first page and admire the font that I know was blocked together on a hand press right in the Woolfs' home in either Richmond or London—suddenly I can't remember where they were in 1927.

"Yes, of course, if it's fine tomorrow," said Mrs. Ramsay. "But you'll have to be up with the lark," she added.

To her son these words conveyed an extraordinary joy, as if it were settled, the expedition were bound to take place, and the wonder to which he had looked forward, for years and years it seemed, was, after a night's darkness and a day's sail, within touch. Since he belonged, even at the age of six, to that great clan which cannot keep this feeling separate from that, but must let future prospects, with their joys and sorrows, cloud what is actually at hand, since to such people even in earliest childhood any turn in the wheel of sensation has the power to crysallise and transfix the moment upon which its gloom or radiance rests, James Ramsay, sitting on the floor cutting out pictures from the illustrated catalogue of the Army and Navy stores, endowed the picture of a refrigerator, as his mother spoke, with heavenly bliss. It was fringed with joy. The wheelbarrow, the lawnmower, the sound of poplar trees, leaves whitening before the rain, rooks cawing, brooms knocking, dresses rustling—all these were so coloured and distinguished in his mind that he had already his private code, his secret language, though he appeared the image of stark and uncompromising severity, with his high forehead and his fierce blue eyes, impeccably candid and pure, frowning slightly at the sight of human frailty, so that his mother, watching him guide his scissors neatly round the refrigerator, imagined him all red and ermine on the Bench or directing a stern and momentous enterprise in some crisis of public affairs.

"But," said his father, stopping in front of the drawing-room window, "it won't be fine."

The writing is as good as I'd remembered it. So many things happening at once to draw the reader into the story. The magical inner life of childhood and its frustrations with adults and their odd constraints. The middle-class ambitions of mothers, their mild optimisms. The bludgeoning realism of fathers with sons. The low-grade tension between husband and wife. The real possibilities for hope and disappointment—all of this in just a single page. A story (and a book) that has survived and that will live on into the future, regardless of what it may hold.

Why on earth does Thien want to sell it? Especially now.

But, of course, I know the reason. I slowly flip to the inside front cover and discover the offending object. Centered there is a bookplate, white with plain black lettering (no image), identifying the owner as Naomi Mitchison—that is Lady Naomi May Margaret Mitchison, the Scottish novelist, CBE—with her signature and book ownership quotation. From my perspective, the bookplate of a famous novelist and contemporary of Virginia Woolf would add personal value and significance to the text. Something, I should have thought, that Thien could chat about to her literary friends when they visit Kutna Hora. Another name to drop, so to speak. I know I would have been impressed. But this is not how Thien sees it. As far as she's concerned, the bookplate only clutters up the front endpaper. A blemish, I think she once called it. She notices me looking at it now.

"Ms. Mitchison's book still," she says.

"Oh, Thien," I say.

Nevertheless, my mind is already working on the sale. I've got the Swiss collector on the hook for the Fitzgerald, and I don't want to jeopardize that sale, but sometimes when a collector gets giddy with the thrill of acquiring one book, riding that high can compel them into a second purchase. I wonder if Bechtsold would be interested in a Woolf with a literary pedigree?

"Don't 'Oh, Thien' me, Henry. We've had this conversation a half a dozen times."

"I know, I know," I say. "If you really want to know I was already thinking about a potential buyer. A Swiss client of mine."

"Harold Bechtsold?"

"Yes. How would you feel about my approaching him about the sale of your *Lighthouse*?"

Thien arranges her face in a thoughtful expression as if she's considering the relative merits of Harold Bechtsold, though I would swear this is only a little playacting for my benefit.

"I think that would be okay."

"Great."

"He is a wealthy man?" Thien says.

"Well, he buys what he wants when he wants it. And if he has an occupation, I've never been able to detect it."

Thien raises a thoroughly plucked eyebrow. She generally gets what she wants, too, though her most expensive acquisitions have to be approved by her husband. A source, I believe, of tremendous frustration for Thien.

"If it's all right with you, I'll take this with me today then," I say, holding the book against my chest. Now I'm the one being polite, playing the game, so to speak, since we both know that coming for the book and taking it away is why I got on the train this morning. Still, I've had clients change their minds at the last moment, unable to part with a book when it finally came down to it. But not Thien—she has made up her mind.

"Yes, that's fine."

"Good. I'm supposed to see Bechtsold soon."

I open my briefcase and remove a contract for Thien to sign, just a little something saying that she has given me authority to take possession of the book and to act on her behalf to facilitate a sale. In this transaction, I am only the middle man taking his percentage. When Thien signs, I place the *Lighthouse* in a plastic sleeve and then wrap that in a clean white cloth before placing the whole package in my briefcase.

"May I offer you a drink?" Thien says.

"Yes, please."

"I was thinking of a sherry. Wait, no, you prefer scotch, don't you?" Remembering her guests' little preferences is a source of pride for Thien. I know her social life is an active one with many parties and soirees and book-club–like salons, but Kutna Hora is very out of the way and there must be many days, like this one, where nothing is going on. I wonder, despite her loud eccentricities, if she isn't actually very lonely. I look at her now and she seems ageless, as always, but also somehow a little diminished. I realize that in all the time that I've known her, I've never met her husband.

"A scotch on the rocks would be perfect after my climb up the hill," I say, and I can see that Thien is pleased that I've accepted.

I watch her go to a cabinet in the corner and begin to make our drinks. She is a fastidious bartender. There is a slightly awkward silence as I find I don't have anything particularly scintillating to say. That's how Thien makes you feel, as though being witty and not a little charming are prerequisites for being human, for civilization.

When she hands me my drink, I say, "If there is something for you at Nemec's, Morgan and I can email photos to you immediately if you like."

"I was going to ask you to do that, actually," Thien says.

"Wonderful. That's what we'll plan to do."

"I can hardly wait."

For a moment, we sip from our drinks and look out the big windows. This is a beautiful, beautiful room.

"You know that it will be my job to dispose of Nemec's entire collection. To begin with a substantial sale to you will be good for everyone." I don't know why I've said this, revealing so much more about my hopes than I'd intended. But I feel this sudden desire to give something real to Thien, to connect with her as a friend, almost, rather than just as a client. I can tell by the odd expression on her face that she's surprised.

"I'm sure you're going to do wonderful work for them," Thien says.

"Yes, we'll try. Thanks."

As I finish my drink and then slowly gather myself to go, I wonder how Thien became a bibliophile. We all of us have our stories. I have my lonely childhood and Sherlock Holmes and Dena Al-Juhani. What about Thien? Does she have fond memories of being read to by her mother or a sister or a nurse in Hong Gai? Did she have a long illness that kept her confined to bed with nothing but books to help her live? Were books an escape from heavy-handed Communist politics? An illicit glimpse into the West? Was her father a respected librarian? Her taste has never been to my knowledge obviously escapist. Though I suppose no one can really say what might be among the private stash on her bedside table.

Maybe if I find a nice Bloomsbury for her, I'll screw up the courage to ask her. At the front door again, we pause to shake hands.

"I'll be checking my email every hour, Henry Marten. Don't keep me waiting!" Thien says.

"I won't!" I say. "Good-bye."

Thien's door closes behind me and I crunch my way along the gravel drive, down the hill into Kutna Hora and the train station.

Descending the hill, my strides lengthened by gravity, I feel a sudden and sickening vertigo so powerful that I have to stop and support myself along a low stone wall. Without meaning to, my head, already spinning, conjures up images of myself as a child with Dena who is now not a child any longer but a grown woman, nearly forty years old, with children of her own and a body altered by time and experience. I am nauseated by the swift passage of time, the careening, sparking transit of a life that moves so quickly that it feels impossible to take stock. And what frightens me, *is frightening me*, is the way that possibility turns into fact, gets branded into a history that can't be shaken off or rewritten regardless of future action. That Dena and I simply drifted apart and walked away from the attractions of beautiful, tragic love. That Stephanie has lost her girlishness and not a little of her romantic idealism to become a Professional, dressed in black, moving world events. That Michael and Anna have lost their fortune. That Selma's husband has been arrested by the government of the United States and been taken from her, and that this event has infected her body like a cancer, ravaging her life, changing her, so that she will never again be the same. Most horrifying of all, though, is the constant knowledge that my hand is in all of these things, a variable of greater or lesser value, that can affect the direction of so many lives, most especially my own. The great desire to not fuck things up, made even more potent by the idea that my excuses not to act well are so few, enlarged no doubt in my mind by so much literature, by so many narratives to do something great because I can. Because at the very least, my life should be a great story.

The station at last. Sit yourself down, open the window. Let everything go for a little while, let the train take you slowly back to Prague.

———

Stephanie has show tunes blasting on the stereo when I return and is dancing a little jig with the index finger of each hand pumping up and down to punctuate the steps. She smiles maniacally.

"I guess you've had a good day," I say. Despite myself, I have not once thought of my wife's interaction with real Western power or, at least, the Assistant Secretary of State.

"One of the best," she says. She's mixing Negronis. Do I want one? I do. She's wearing only a blue camisole and a black thong. Her power suit lies discarded in a puddle beside the couch.

"The Czechs never fail to surprise me," she says. "A decades-long history of subversion and they still jump to attention the moment any real authority shows up."

"Meaning what?"

"Meaning that it looks like they're going to accept the radar system as long as the actual missiles are in Poland."

I place my briefcase with Thien's *Lighthouse* onto a chair and then remove my jacket and very carefully, as is my custom, roll up my shirtsleeves to just below the elbow.

"That's wonderful," I say. "I think."

"Well," she says. "It's what we want."

I can hear her pouring the gin and Campari into the shaker. In another moment she will add the ice cubes, slice a lime. Another little ritual, another marker of civilization—a drink being mixed in the European evening.

"Where's Selma?"

"She's doing a follow-up with Anthony and Belinda. Apparently Miss New York Times was just sober enough last night to know she was too drunk to interview Selma properly."

"They're really going to write a story about Mansour?"

"So it would seem."

"I'm worried," I say, "that this is going to get Selma's hopes up."

"I told you, she's a big girl. I'm sure she knows what she's doing."

No. She's fragile and at the end of her rope. She's nearly broken. Can't you see that? Surely, a power broker of the Western world ought to be able to see the obvious.

"That's what you keep saying." Stephanie slices a lime and the fragrance seems to fill the room. I can feel a tingling anticipation of the drink in the back of my throat and wonder, not for the first time, if I've started drinking too much.

"Well, she called this afternoon," Stephanie says, "to tell me what she was doing. She sounded very happy, very upbeat. She said coming to Prague was lucky. She's been here hardly any time at all and already good things are happening."

"I guess there's no arguing that," I say.

"And yet? And still? You're convinced that this is some mirage and when the story runs and nothing happens Selma will collapse into a big ball of despair."

"Something like that."

"Henry Marten, you are very seriously in danger of fucking up my good mood."

"Sorry."

"Don't be. I love that you care so much."

Stephanie shakes the Negronis and when she does it, she puts her whole body into it, shaking her boobs, which lie loose under the thin cami. I don't know whether to watch her or the red liquid pouring into the cocktail glasses. I think of all the men at the embassy who must admire her, a woman of action, brokering deals and mixing drinks. I wonder at the subtle ways she uses her sexuality to get what she wants. Or if she plays it straight? A little bit like Clark Kent wanting to succeed as a journalist without the benefit of his Superman powers. Heh, someday when we're very drunk and happy together, I will ask her if she's Clark Kent. But not today.

"Though I have to tell you," she says, handing me my drink, "that we might both be a little bit in danger of becoming Selma-obsessed."

"Is that condition in the *DSM-IV*?"

"It's slated for the new edition."

"Mmm. This Negroni is delicious."

"Thanks. But I mean, really, ever since she's arrived I feel like we've suddenly inherited someone's unstable teenage daughter." Stephanie takes a healthy sip of her drink. "Please don't ever tell anyone I said that."

"You're safe with me," I say and smile. "Okay, then. Tell me about the Assistant Secretary."

We sit down on the couch together and she squirms happily into the leather cushion, getting comfortable, excited to dish some of the gossipy details of her day to someone who won't hold anything against her.

"I don't know how some people do it, you know. They just ooze charisma. He's maybe fifty-five, but he's one of those men who will be wiry thin their whole lives with a thick, full head of hair. It's so juvenile but I literally spent half the day looking at this man's hair. Sometimes I think something's wrong with me."

"There's nothing wrong with you. I'm sure you were thinking about radar systems when you weren't thinking about his hair."

"Mostly. It was so impressive."

"His hair again?"

"Yes, but no. I meant the way he had the Czechs eating out of his hand. I don't think I've ever seen anything like it. But he's a little sickening, too. He's one of those Ivy League pedigree types who went to prep schools that you've only read about in novels and then Yale and then Harvard's public policy school. Still, it's not as though he acts like a snob."

"Our best and brightest."

"He might *actually* be, you know? I kept waiting all day for some part of him to crack open and reveal all the evil nastiness."

"But it never did?"

"Not today anyway."

"Okay, I'll play," I say after a moment's pause. "Why do we want a radar-controlled missile system in Central Europe?"

"There are a lot of reasons, but it really just boils down to two." Stephanie flashes me the peace sign with the hand not actively engaged with her Negroni. "It provides military deterrence in Europe of the kind that we used to have in Germany during the Cold War but that they're unwilling to sponsor any longer. And, it puts a more direct military role in the hands of NATO, especially into the hands of new members like the Czech Republic and Poland."

"Time to pull your own weight and all that."

Stephanie looks at me suspiciously because she can't quite tell if there was an edge of sarcasm in my comment or not.

"Right," she says. "They cc'd you on the memo?"

We both laugh, but underneath the jokiness is an edge of something else. Probably she thinks I meant nothing by the comment, but I can see that the idea that I might have been pushing against the embassy's official position, *needling* her as one of its leading spokesmen, well, that would be a new wrinkle in the life of our marriage. And how often does that happen? How often does a spouse actually surprise you?

But Stephanie is a cool customer. If all of a sudden I've developed a political consciousness, especially one that might be opposed to her own, she won't try to discover the details by direct interrogation. It will be much more subtle.

"No," I say, "but you talk in your sleep."

She laughs again and I laugh, too, as I watch her nose disappear deep into her cocktail glass.

"Aren't you hungry for dinner?" she says when she resurfaces.

"I could eat."

"Let's just order something from the Kafka. I don't think I can pull anything else together."

"You know I'd eat there every day if you let me."

"But I wouldn't because you'd become fat and your arteries would clog and get high blood pressure and have a stroke or a heart attack and die right in the middle of good sex or something."

"I'm glad to see it all really boils down to your orgasm," I say.

"Fuck you," she says.

"Right. That's what I said."

Stephanie picks up the phone and calls downstairs and places an order for both of us without asking what I want. It's a game we play, to see if we can guess what the other's hungry for.

"Twenty minutes," she says when she hangs up the phone. "Tell me about Thien and her book."

"It's beautiful. Would you like to see it?"

I don't wait for her to answer but get up with my drink and remove *To the Lighthouse* from my briefcase. I hand it to Stephanie and watch her carefully unwrap it from its plastic sheath. Suddenly we are two people in various states of undress, drinking cocktails with a nearly $20,000 book between us.

"Wow," she says. "Now that I see it, I can't believe Thien Diep wants to sell." She flips open to a random page and lowers her head to smell the paper. A true bookseller's wife.

"Watch your drink," I say. Stephanie's glass has begun to sweat and I have visions of little droplets warping the almost hundred-year-old pages.

"Henry?" Stephanie says, and it's so odd to hear her actually address me by my name. Without exactly knowing it, I sit up a little straighter, raise my chin half an inch.

"Yes, love?"

"What if you're right?"

"About what? Thien?"

"No. About Selma." Stephanie places the book on the coffee table and sips a little self-consciously at her drink. She leans back into the couch and sighs. "This is going to sound stupid, but there's something not right when I look at her. You know, really look at her."

"She's had a terrible experience," I say. "She's still having it."

When Stephanie nods, there is something so solemn in it that I wish I had just agreed with her easy optimism about Selma. I can't help but feel that it is my skepticism that's helped something dark grow inside my wife's mind.

"That's just it. What if she melts down, here in Prague? With us? Everything has just been so weird. Her showing up a day early. And I've been distracted by the Assistant Secretary."

"I'm worried about her, too. But whatever happens, it won't be your fault."

"I know. There's just this vibe coming off Selma. She's like one of those rotating billboards: pathetic one moment, almost dangerous the next."

"Yes," I say.

"You see it, too."

"Let's just say I know what you're talking about."

In fact, I've already envisioned all matter of dark and unhappy drama. Selma enduring the three and a half days when Mansour effectively disappeared, arrested by the FBI and then simply falling into some kind of Homeland Security black hole. Selma sitting in the beautifully appointed lounge outside her attorney's office, picking, picking, picking the polish from her nails. Selma entering the prison where they're holding her husband, being startled by the smells of cold metal and cement and something identifiably human but foul. Selma sitting across a plexiglass divide from Mansour, the deep shadows under his eyes, the rough stubble growing like weeds on his normally smooth skin, his eyeglasses ever so slightly bent. Selma thinking that she is a character in a TV drama and not a real person, but then driving home again and lying on her bed and realizing that all of this is far too real. Selma spending days in that bed, the sheets growing rank with her sweat, curled, unmoving, into the smallest shape she can contrive, not daring to utter a single word, afraid to be discovered herself, the only sign that she's alive her eyes that follow the path of the sun and shadow across the walls and inter-mittently leak tears. And then: Selma making the endless phone calls, Selma studying minutely every proviso in the Patriot Act, Selma organizing petitions, Selma spending hours in NYU's Law Library searching and searching for new strategies to

recommend to the attorneys. Selma getting on a plane and hur-
dling through space and time to land here, in Prague.

Who is this Selma Al-Khateeb who has arrived to stay with
us? Surely not the charming friend that Stephanie remembers
from D.C. Instead, there is a woman who seeks favor and
opportunity. Who is prepared to play husband against wife.
Who, seemingly, without a thought embroils herself with the
national press of two nations. Who drinks alcohol, who no
longer prays. Who has become the object of my deepest sexual
fantasies. And that's really where my mind is, searching out
into the evening for Selma.

"The timing is horrible," Stephanie says. "Normally, it would
be no problem to take a few days off and just be with her."

I knock back the last of my Negroni and nod.

"Listen. I can't be with her, but you can," she says. "That
was always part of the plan anyway, right?"

"Right."

"Then take her with you when you go to see Anna's uncle."

"To Brno? I was going to take Morgan. And we're staying
overnight."

"Look, no offense, but what you guys do isn't exactly rocket
science. Besides, you're just cataloging the books. If I know
you and Morgan, you'll spend half of your time scouring Brno
for the best pubs."

"That is certainly part of our diabolical plan."

"Then take Selma with you instead. She can help you catalogue the books just as well as Morgan, plus she'll think it's
great fun, a kind of literary adventure."

"It wouldn't be the same as Morgan. She doesn't have the slightest ability to evaluate a book," I say. "All she'll be able to do is record what I tell her."

"Does it really matter? This is just what Selma said she wanted. She'll be completely absorbed by it."

"Morgan's going to be pissed."

"He'll get over it. And if the uncle becomes difficult about anything, it never hurts to have a beautiful woman around to keep everyone on their best behavior."

"You think beautiful women inspire good behavior?"

"Well, sometimes." Stephanie smiles, showing me all of her teeth.

I can see that she knows she has me, that I will agree to take Selma to see Milos Nemec. She was worried a moment ago, almost depressed, but now her whole body has reanimated just like it was when I walked through the door and saw her dancing to show tunes. Perhaps she feels good because she's done something. There was a problem: Selma. It needed a solution: Brno. Now it's safe to enjoy today's professional victories.

"Sure," I say. "Sure, I'll take her with me. Though I should make you tell Morgan that he's not coming."

"Oh, no, that's bookstore business. Far be it for me to interfere."

She is laughing now and, once again, I laugh with her. "Go make us another drink," I say and hand her my glass.

I follow the movement of my wife's bare ass when she goes to the kitchen to mix a second round. Things are good here. She's a good woman. Smart, funny, attractive. We have money.

We're happy. I look around the apartment and think only what is obvious: We have a nice life. Why on earth would I want to ruin it? I would not. And yet already I feel myself forcefully tamping down a rising excitement. *Don't send us to Brno together, darling*, I think to say. In fact, I do say it aloud but at a whisper to test what the words would feel like if I actually spoke them to my wife. "Don't send us off together."

"What?" Stephanie calls from the kitchen.

"Nothing," I say. "Just talking to myself."

"Oh, my."

Stephanie's back quickly and hands me a fresh Negroni. We clink glasses and say, "*Na zdraví.*" And for a while I say nothing further at all, which is but a fraction of all that I might if I weren't such a coward.

When Selma returns, Stephanie has already been in bed for two hours. We have given her a key and she lets herself in. I am sitting on the couch in my boxers and a T-shirt and what had made me anxious this morning doesn't even really register with me now. Selma can discover me in any state she likes. I have been staring out the window at the lights in the apartment across the street and I don't look away until Selma has been standing in the room for at least half a minute.

I know what I'm looking at. What are you looking at, Selma?

Her presence changes the room. And in truth, I can smell the booze on her from ten feet away. Eventually, she drops her purse like a stone onto the floor and flops down on the couch beside me.

She is sitting very close, her thigh touching mine, her shoulder warming the fabric of my T-shirt. She says nothing and neither do I. In a little while a long, weary sigh escapes her body and she lets her weight rest against me.

"Hi," I say.

"Hello, Henry."

"You okay?"

"Mmm-hmm."

Where have you been, madam? But of course I don't ask. Instead, I watch helplessly as she leans her head against mine. I take a deep breath of the space we're now sharing. There is her hair smelling of sunshine and cigarettes and the faint floral scent from her morning shampoo. The alcohol smells like scotch or bourbon—something brown. Behind it, her breath is a little stale.

Well, Selma, did you get your story? At what price? Has it been paid in full, or will you have to meet them again and again to secure just the right language. Or can you simply tease Anthony—or perhaps Belinda—with the mere promise of access to your life. Or am I simply dying the slow starvation of the undeclared lover, convulsing with the poison of my own bitter imaginings.

"Do you want to go with me to Brno tomorrow?"

Selma turns her head to look at my eyes. "To catalogue the collection?"

"Yes. We'll be gone overnight. Nemec has invited us to stay

at his house." She looks at me again, at my eyes, and then nods.

Okay. We're going then. And isn't that really what I wanted? I didn't really want to come to my senses and I know I didn't want Selma to come to hers on my behalf. What I want is for Selma to love me. It almost doesn't matter to me how she loves me, but certainly not as a husband. She has one of those and I am already someone's husband. Not just as a friend who has done a good turn. Something unforgettable to her. I want her to let me help her, to sacrifice something important that will change things for her, so that when she is an old woman giving wisdom to a small child she will think of me and say to her, "Find a man who will lay himself down for you, who knows how to give to you instead of only to take." I want to do something so powerful for this woman that I will cease to be just a man to her but become an idea.

"Tomorrow may be quite a day," I say. "We better get some sleep."

Eight

The train from Prague to Brno is much like the one to Kutna Hora—at least once the un-beautiful outer edges of the city fall away and we break into the countryside. I want Selma to have the full experience, and so to feel like real Czechs we buy ham sandwiches from the little counter at the station to eat during the trip. The green fields pass by, the white houses with their red tiled roofs, only the occasional satellite dish marring the scene. Selma sits in the seat across from me, and strands of her hair blow lazily from the breeze coming through the open window. It's early in the morning and neither of us has yet had much to say. I find that I'm very content looking across at her lovely face, appearing just a little older and more vulnerable in the direct, early morning sun, one cheek still faintly lined from her pillow.

Selma has brought along the copy of *Possession*, but it remains unopened in her lap. One palm rests carelessly across the cover.

"Have you read that before?" I say. No, she hasn't. She's seen the film.

"The opening scene is in the Reading Room of the London Library."

"Mmm."

"Mmm, is right. And we will soon be in a beautiful library as well. Getting ready to make who-knows-what discoveries."

"You're excited, aren't you?" she asks.

I nod and we exchange a genuine, uncomplicated smile. Though after a moment or two we return to our landscape vigil. The swaying of the train is gentle and friendly-seeming.

"When we get there," Selma says, "what will the work be like?" She doesn't look at me when she says this, just continues to gaze out the window.

"The main job will be to catalogue the books. I have a template and a spreadsheet on my laptop. I thought that I could examine each title and then you can type in the details as I tell them to you. That's how Morgan and I usually work."

"Great."

"Is it?"

"Yes," she says. "It sounds wonderfully mindless."

Is that what she thinks of my work? Donkey tricks? Something that even a reasonably trained specimen could do without too much difficulty? More likely, she's played out and wants to forget herself, forget that Mansour is in jail.

"You're not going to ask Stephanie to help Mansour, are you?" Selma says.

The subject change makes me sit up a little straighter.

"I was hoping, actually, that you were going to tell me that I didn't need to bother."

Selma's face flattens out in an incomprehensible expression. "You know," I add, "Anthony and Belinda."

"I *need* Stephanie's help."

"You're convinced of this?"

"Yes. The publicity will be nice if Belinda's article runs in the *Times*, but I told you: Mansour is going to die in there. If something isn't done quickly, then— " Her hands jump into the air and then fall again like birds shot from the sky mid-flight.

"Listen, don't be angry with me. What I'm about to say is meant in the kindest possible way." I don't go on until Selma nods her head—halfhearted at best. "Don't you think you're being dramatic?"

My reward is a long, dull-eyed look. Then a small smile.

"If I were you, Henry, I would say to you the same thing."

"But you're not me."

"No."

Selma stands up and makes a long stretch like one of the cats from Coventry Drive. Then she sits beside me, loops her arm under mine, and rests her head on my shoulder. And, as always, these easy gestures of intimacy are disarming. The warmth of her skin against my shoulder, the scent of her hair. Sometimes I wonder what it must feel like to be aware of your own charms and to stand outside of yourself, even briefly, and watch yourself using them. Does it feel like a game? Is it invigorating, electric, like power coursing through a transformer? Or is it such a parody of something sincere that it makes her sad? The real Selma must lurk somewhere beneath all these layers.

"I am so unspeakably fucked up," she says. There's a kind of playfulness to her voice, but it's also clear she means it. "I feel like a child who is about to jump from a merry-go-round that keeps spinning faster and faster."

She looks up at me to see if I'm listening or listening properly. When I nod she rests her head on my shoulder again.

"The problem is that I know I have to jump. I have to take some action, make a decision—and fast. I can't stop thinking of the last time I saw Mansour. I sat in my car after I left the jail and thought I was going to be sick. He's such a beautiful man, and they're killing him. *Killing him.* You didn't see him, Henry. He's so thin and he has these bright red rings around his eyes like he hasn't slept in a thousand years. I can feel it here," she says, rubbing her stomach. "It's a stone that never goes away. If I don't do something now, my husband is going to die."

I lean my head against hers. For a moment, I let her words linger in the air of the train with us. When the atmosphere seems to be still again, I say, "You're just played out, Selma. I would be, too. Remember that you're supposed to be in Prague to forget all of this, if only for a little while."

Selma laughs and the sound is an ugly one. "It doesn't seem to be working."

"Have you seen anyone about this? A doctor, I mean."

"A psychiatrist?"

"Yeah, I guess so. They could give you something maybe."

She points at her purse sitting on the seat across from us. "There's a pill bottle in there the size of my fist."

"Right," I say. And I'd like to say more but find I'm running low on the material of sympathy and conciliation.

"I'm not really asking for much," Selma says. "I'm not asking to be rich or to discover the talent to be a great genius. All I want to do is to be allowed to live quietly with my husband, in our own house. I want to cook him dinner and suggest books for him to read. We used to take long walks together, Henry. Five, six miles through the city. Just watching people, stopping to sit on a bench, buy a coffee. He is the gentlest man. That's what I can't let go of . . . the absurdity."

"So you really think Stephanie can help?"

"Here is what I think: Somewhere there's a room that only a few people have access to. Not even especially important people, mind you. And in that room is a lever. All that has to happen is for one of those not-so-important people to pull that lever. Then my husband can come home."

Was this right? Had Selma whittled the situation down to some nugget of truth? Perhaps all that had to happen was for the people holding Mansour to decide that he wasn't a risk—a thing that could happen just as abruptly and mysteriously as his arrest. Or perhaps it was just pretty to think so.

When we leave the train there is a solemn-faced man holding
a handwritten placard with my name on it, like something out
of a movie. Selma sees him first, and when she nudges me with
an elbow, I enjoy the sight of her real smile again. And there is
something wonderful about being met like this, being expected.
Maybe it even raises me in her esteem. I am a man who is met at
train stations. The man's name is Georg, and he has almost no
English. My Czech is just enough to understand, as he leads us
to a black Mercedes, that he works for Uncle Nemec.

Georg first drives us through historical Brno with its cobblestone streets. We see the Cathedral of Saints Peter and
Paul, its spire piercing the cobalt-blue sky like a lance or
javelin; the red-and-white trams that hiss quietly along, just
like those in Prague; the architecture of the past, *the past*,
smoothing out the jangled edges of my nerves just by looking
at it. Here the modern world is almost kept at bay, though
not so well as in Prague. In Brno, it's possible to turn in the
wrong direction and see new high-rise business complexes,
all steel and glass, crowding their way into the old world.
But before I can let this upset my fantasy of Brno, Georg is
taking us through the Pisárky Tunnel and outside the city
where Nemec has his house.

Before I am ready, in fact, we are making our slow way up a
steep hillside and along a gravel drive. If the house is anything
to go by, Uncle Nemec is still a rich man despite his losses. It
is not some palatial estate left over from the Margraviate of

Moravia but a house, like Thien Diep's—though it is a large, architecturally complex one.

It's not the home of the king but of a local lord, a place where the family's sons grow up to be knights and die honorably in battle or live and grow old in the position of magistrate of this or that principality. The outside is white stone, the roof red tile. It's shaped, roughly, in an L with rounded three-story towers at the ends and corner. The gravel drive finishes in a turnaround marked by the ubiquitous cherub peeing noisily into his basin. And the red-and-white striped flag of the city flies over a set of wide, iron-fitted double doors. The house strikes me suddenly as the perfect place for one of Agatha Christie's Poirot murder mysteries. One where Poirot has just taken the *Orient Express* and then been diverted on his way to Istanbul by a telegram from the daughter of an old friend begging for his help. Before it is too late.

Most importantly, the house has absolutely nothing of the New Jersey prison about it. No dingy waiting areas or plexiglass visitation stations that haven't been updated since the early '80s. If ever there was a chance for Selma to let go of her troubles, even for a bit, this might be the place.

Georg puts the Mercedes in park and, for a moment, no one moves or speaks. The three of us just sit there quietly with the engine ticking, a little hesitant to make the next move. But then Georg is opening Selma's door for her and I'm out, too, walking now as a group toward those impressive double doors. With Selma beside me I ring the doorbell, while Georg sees to the luggage from the trunk. My hands are shaking a bit, uneasy

suddenly to meet Uncle Nemec and almost beside myself with
desire to lay my eyes and hands upon those books.

Marketa opens the door to us. This is Nemec's housekeeper.
She is plump, pinch-faced, and lost somewhere in her forties or
fifties. She wears a very sensible beige dress, very sensible black
shoes. For some reason I immediately think of Virginia Woolf's
housekeeper, Nellie, who caused so many ambivalent feelings
in her employers. I don't know why I should be thinking of
Nellie, as I've never seen a photograph of her, though it might
be a projection of how much I'm hoping to find a Bloomsbury
for Thien Diep.

"Good afternoon," she says in heavily accented English.
"You are Mister Henry Marten?"

"Yes. And this is my assistant, Selma Al-Khateeb."

"Please come in," she says, but she's looking at Selma with
great interest.

I am not disappointed by my first glimpse of the house.
The entry, as will be true of most of the house, is vaulted like
a 16th-century church, a skein of rough plaster, painted white,
covering the ribs and joints. The floor is tiled in brown and
maroon. Two faded brass pots hold giant palms that stand sentinel just inside the door. The room is spotless and there is the
slight scent of lemon in the air. It is as though the house has
reached out a hand to shake ours, perhaps condescended a little
bow of greeting.

Marketa leads us into a sitting room at the front of the house,
and I risk a quick look at Selma, who arches her eyebrows and
smirks. I can't tell if she's impressed or just pretending to be,

but she looks at ease. She looks engaged. She looks as though she's *here*.

I have to remind myself that it doesn't matter whether Selma actually cares about what we're doing here today or not. This is a onetime thing. She is not my employee or a new partner. I am not teaching her the business. I'm just helping a friend. More importantly I am helping *my wife's* friend — a kind of Bring the Psychologically Damaged to Work Day. Therapy. Like the man who attended to the porphyria-related madness of England's George III and who prescribed labor and routine as the best cure for mental illness. Though it would be nice if she cared, if in a little while we'll be led into a cool room where row upon row of books stretch out before us, and that those seemingly endless possibilities make Selma's heart jump in her chest, joyous, like a child on a trampoline. Because then maybe — I can't help thinking it, almost like pushing away an unwanted erection by thinking of a brick wall — some of that joy will be transferred to me. In that room, with those books, she will be happy. And it will have been Henry Marten who brought her there.

But first, we wait.

The sitting room has an ornate fireplace with a nest of logs artfully arranged in the grate. And as we sit down to wait for Uncle Nemec on beautifully worn leather sofas, I am convinced that the house, maybe the whole occasion, requires a soundtrack. Dvorak or Janacek, perhaps. Another sensory perception to provide the right amount of gravitas and stamp the day into our minds forever. I then can see just how excited I am, the way that my mind is spooling out like yarn and tangling.

"The house is lovely," I say to Marketa.

"Yes," she says. "Thank you."

Immediately I see this was a mistake. The compliment is not really hers to take, but more, she knows I'm here to make it less beautiful—a hired gun sent to crate up the books and sell them off so that the lights can be kept on and the tea served on time.

"Excuse me," she says. "I will tell Mr. Nemec that you have arrived."

"It is lovely, isn't it?" Selma says when Marketa has disappeared down the hall. "Old. Look at how low the doorway is. From when people were smaller."

I nod, still taking it all in.

"Who are the Nemecs?" she asks. "How did they make their money?"

"I don't really know. All that Michael has ever said is that they are an 'old Czech family.' I think his idea is that we shouldn't know the details. Let our imaginations do their work."

"No doubt our imaginations will be better than reality."

"No doubt that was the plan."

Milos Nemec comes into the room moving much faster than I had expected, a real burst of energy as he ducks slightly under the doorframe. His eyes are cast to the floor, but there's a sly smile on his face, as if he's ever so slightly abashed to admit to some naughty action about which we will soon hear. I wonder if this is his style, a public face, put on like a favorite dinner jacket to make a good first impression. Marketa will show his guests into this beautiful room, soften them—us—up, so to speak, and then *voilà!*, the smiling Milos Nemec will make his entrance.

Brilliant. Of course, I may just be imagining this. Though it is also true that this isn't my first rodeo. I've been in enough beautifully decorated sitting rooms in D.C., in New York, and now in Prague to know that when the wealthy, especially collectors, find themselves in the position where they must sell off their valuables, something has to be done to preserve the right amount of dignity. In this light, the flourish of a small entrance doesn't seem out of the ordinary.

"Hello, Henry Marten, terribly sorry. I was in the library having one last look before you ransack the place."

Nemec is fair, with a white fringe around his otherwise bald pate. He has a very handsome face, I think, except for a hawkish nose that, while not necessarily attractive, adds to the drama of his features. He looks like a man at ease with the elegance of his life, particularly his clothes—a bit like some friends of Stephanie's who attended the Hill School and who always seemed so at ease in their suits and ties, having worn them since the age of ten or eleven. Today, Nemec is dressed in a classic navy blazer with bright brass buttons and gray pants. His tie, knotted in a Windsor, is maroon and gray. He reminds me of Prince Philip, Duke of Edinburgh, a comparison I suspect he'd appreciate.

I offer my hand and we shake, me grinning like a monkey all the while. "Hopefully the process will be a little more gentle than that."

"Of course, of course," he says. "I meant nothing by it. Only that I'll be sad to see them go."

Though Milos Nemec doesn't look particularly sad.

"Mr. Nemec, this is Selma Al-Khateeb. Selma is visiting from

the United States and thought she'd like to see a little of how
the book business works."

"Ah, how charming," Nemec says as he looks Selma up and
down, lingering a moment on the curve of her left breast. It's
a demonstration of hunger I don't think I could ever show in
public.

"You're home is so beautiful," Selma says. "It's a wonderful
privilege to be here." Nemec points to me and flashes, once
again, that sly smile.

"Henry, you are one smart cookie," he says, trying on this
American expression, "to bring along such a lovely assistant to
soften the blow. By the time she's through with me, I will have
agreed to sell everything in the house!"

He does a quick turn and raises his arms above his head and
waves them about dramatically as if to encompass the walls, the
ceiling, the very air before us. The effort, when he turns around
again, has turned his cheeks a rosy pink.

And right on cue, Selma laughs a tinkling, giggling girlish
laugh, perfect for the moment and for Uncle Nemec's ego. I
laugh, too, but am beside the point—a place I'm suddenly very
content to be. A different woman would have taken offense at
the old man's lasciviousness, but not Selma. Is it simply that
she knows there are greater things at stake and doesn't mind
using her beauty to acquire what she wants—in this case, God
bless her, to help me? Or has her life taught her a new kind of
empathy? Perhaps she now lives in a world where the proper
response to dirty old men is simply pity. Either case over-
whelms me.

"May I offer you two a drink?" Nemec says. "It's maybe too early for a brandy, but perhaps a cool glass of white wine to take the edge off your journey?"

"That would be lovely," Selma answers for us. I nod.

"Perfect! I'll tell Marketa to bring it to us in the library."

Nemec leads us through the low doorway, down a long hallway to the back of the house, and into the library, chatting flirtatiously with Selma as we go. I fall a step or two behind in order to watch them. I think if someone suddenly presented him with a spoon, Nemec would eat her with it. As it is, he may simply have to use his teeth.

He says to Selma, his voice faux rueful and sad, "Perhaps you have heard that I have been unlucky? Risky investments. The Wheel of Fortune, you know. And so I must liquidate."

Selma places her hand on his arm as we walk. "I'm sure it's just a temporary setback. Sometimes we need adversity to show us who we really are."

"Henry." Nemec slows and half-turns to look at me. "You should hold on to this one. She is very wise."

"I know. I feel lucky to have her with me."

"Maybe when you have your nose in a book, Henry, I will come and steal her away. I could use someone to show me who I really am."

Selma and I laugh, though it comes out sounding like the music from a broken carousel: wheezing, distorted. Nemec does not laugh at all, not even his signature sly smile.

Simmer down, Uncle Nemec. We're here to look at your books, not test your Viagra prescription.

We reach a broad wooden door fashioned with horizontal iron bands, the rough-hewn wood smoothed dark with age. Nemec swings the door wide, and there it is. The library. Despite the fact that we're here to see the books, the most prominent feature of the room is a bank of windows that gives a view of the garden beyond and swells the room with sunlight. It is a spectacular effect. Especially as the beams of light lead the eye across the room to three walls of shelving and, of course, the books standing like little soldiers, their chests puffed out, ready for inspection.

As always, it is even better than I imagined.

This may be the perfect moment to see this library. The sun warming the rugs, making the wood in the room gleam, the black leather of two club chairs looking almost alive. And the smell, of course, like an old friend: dust, vanilla from the incrementally decaying paper. The way the room has an extra layer of quietude, and the feeling that by opening the door a seal has been broken. Preserved between the covers of these books are tens of thousands of pages of human beings' greatest intimacies. Our hopes. Our failures. Our petty dramas. The moment, almost like a crescendo, where we have broken through to some achievement or state of grace.

"Breathtaking," I say.

"I don't know what I will put on the shelves when your work is done," Nemec replies.

"You've absolutely made up your mind about this? Just say the word and we'll get on the next train and return to Prague."

"No, no," he says. "These were my wife's books. Perhaps

it's time to finally turn the page, so to speak. Besides, Anna has bought me a Kindle for my name day. I've decided to join the modern age."

"Right," I say, but can't help feeling like an opportunist. Does Selma feel it, too?

It is at this moment that Marketa brings in the wine, and we are privileged to a demonstration of Uncle Nemec's expertise with a cork. The gentle "pop," the sound of the Riesling pouring in, the obvious pleasure it gives to him to offer each of us a glass.

"Let's have a toast then," he says. "To beautiful women and expensive books." We are treated once again to Selma's charming laugh, and we both repeat the toast. Nemec is all smiles.

"This is fantastic wine," I say.

"Yes, it's a favorite."

Selma wanders away from us, across the room to the bank of windows with its view of the garden. Nemec watches her move with appreciation and says, "Who is this woman?"

"She's a friend of my wife's. Her husband is in prison in the States, a Patriot Act thing, if you understand me."

"Yes. Sadly, Czechs know all too well these kinds of things."

Nemec might want to know more, but I believe he's right and understands the situation perfectly. I don't know anything about this family's past, but certainly they found themselves on one side or the other of a society where nearly everyone could be an informant for the government and often was. In fact, he probably understands things so well that his most important response would be to laugh at our naïveté.

Something vague and unpleasant moves through Nemec's expression. It's possible he simply feels great sympathy for a beautiful woman's troubles, but it's also just as likely that the disappointment is personal. Fifteen years after the Velvet Revolution it has become painfully clear that there is no such thing as happiness, not for countries, and that the best that can be hoped for is to sustain the daydream of future happiness, that we're on the right path. Otherwise—and this is maybe the look I see on Nemec's face—we're all just Gregor Samsas waiting to discover our ugly transformations. Better to make a little money, Nemec no doubt believes, with which to more easily stave off the inevitable.

Under such conditions, what good are three walls full of books to a man like him? Perhaps there will be a little pain, a pang or two of regret having to do with the memory of his wife, when the books are gone, but nothing that will last too long.

I bet his empty shelves will become a story he tells at parties. *Look*, he might say, *and see what happens when you gamble with the Russians. Those scorpions.*

And all Nemec's guests will laugh and think him worldly, a figure of rich experiences. I can see it all so clearly.

For a moment, Nemec and I stand together and watch Selma gaze out the window. Because I frame the world through books, I think of us as two minor characters taking in the bright light of a (doomed?) heroine, waiting to see how her next move will set our lives spinning.

Nemec puts his hand on my shoulder and says quietly, "Why don't I leave the two of you to this work. You'll have dinner with me later. I'll send Marketa to you at some point to show you where you'll sleep."

There must be something in the air here that Nemec believes he's perceived. It dawns on me that he must think that Selma and I are lovers. And that a moment has presented itself.

There is in his words just the faintest trace of resignation, a benign jealousy, and at the same time a vicarious pleasure at the idea of my success with this beauty. Like an old Polonius, perhaps he hopes to hide behind a curtain and watch something poignant unfold. I don't have the heart to disappoint him.

"That sounds great. Making a catalogue of the collection isn't difficult but it is time consuming. Best to get to it," I say, and can't help but feel that it's all bullshit, just chatter that gets us from point *a* to point *b*, but that everyone knows, especially old Nemec, is hiding some more intimate truth, and that he and I—*as men*—are somehow in collusion together.

"Until dinner, then," he says loudly enough that Selma turns around and smiles her good-bye to him.

When the door closes behind him, I say, "Well, here we are."

"He's quite a character," Selma says.

"Michael did warn me."

"I find him charming," she says.

"Good. You've been incredibly gracious."

"And look, here are all the books!"

There is a breath taken then, the two of us alone in the library of this house in Brno looking at the rows of books, and in that breath something happens. An understanding that neither of us can fathom exactly who we are at this moment or how we arrived here. Selma is both free of her husband's fate and hopelessly tied to it and I have to admit that in these last days—perhaps even from the moment I opened the door to my bedroom and saw that look of horror on Selma's face—something has cracked open in my life. I realize that it still doesn't have to mean anything, that I can still go back from where we are, but that also something truly unexpected might come of standing together in this beautiful room with the sun pouring in the windows.

Selma knows all this, too. I can see it in her face. How easy it would be to talk to her about it, just open my mouth and let all these thoughts out into the open. The idea of being perfectly understood by another, and that that person should be Selma Al-Khateeb! Well.

What I say is, "Valuing a collection can be tricky."

"Can it?"

"Yes. There's a part of me that thinks I'm still a little bit too young for this part of the business. I still get far too excited, and excitement sometimes means overvaluing a title. The problem is that I can't stop thinking about them as sacred artifacts. On some level it would be better if I thought of them as widgets."

"What level would that be?" Selma says. "Let's not go to it."

At this remark I can do nothing but smile and shake my head a little.

"Let's take a first look through the collection," I finally say, because we really should get started.

We walk side by side, starting along the left of the large, U-shaped wall of shelving with their rows and rows of books, the covers looking like someone has cast upon them an enormous handful of confetti. Immediately, we see that the collection has been alphabetized.

As we begin our first slow transit of the room, I say to Selma, "This is the moment when I really have to try to control myself. Otherwise I can fall in love with the idea of a collection. It's actually very unlikely to find a sensation."

"I assumed that."

"I'm just saying this might turn out to be a little disappointing for you."

"Why would I be disappointed?"

"Because it's easy to be. That's all."

We have stopped to run our eyes systematically along the first case. I can smell her perfume and the faint scent of her body after a long morning of travel.

"Look," she says. "*Winesburg, Ohio.*"

"Malcolm Cowley," I say. "*Exile's Return.* Do you know him?"

Selma nods. "I want to say something to you," she says.

"All right."

She smiles. "It's difficult to talk about."

"It doesn't have to be. You should know that by now."

"Should I?"

There's a kind of sad playfulness to her voice. A voice that wants to be flirtatious but can't quite manage it.

Without warning, a wind kicks up and blows open a window across the room. The sharp noise when the casement pops open makes us both jump, then laugh. I begin to roll up the sleeves of my shirt as I walk across the room to shut it, then decide instead to open the window wide. With my back to her, I pick up our conversation.

"You and I have become used to difficult conversations. So just say it."

"I've decided that my life lacks all possibility for certainty. I know that's true of everyone to some extent. But I think most people find ways to make important decisions in their lives; there's something that makes them choose to attend Harvard over Stanford or date Brandon instead of Phillip. I think, usually, there are rules to follow: parental advice, the law, some sacred text. What happens, though, when you think every choice is the wrong one?"

I wait for a moment to see if there's more, but I can see now that she wants an answer.

"You can't know if a choice is wrong until you've acted on it," I say. "The moment you take an action the variables of a decision shift. Sometimes you just have to do something to see your way forward."

Selma tilts her head a little to one side and her expression says *Clever, Henry, but empty*. She moves again to stand by the window that looks out to the garden.

"You know why that advice doesn't work for me?"

"Why?"

"Because I'm not a person anymore."

"I don't know what that means," I say. "Be sensible."

"How can I? When nothing makes sense. You know those things I just said? Parents, government, religion—that's just another way to say society. Normally they work to keep us happily working away within certain lines. A framework, right? But over this last year, since they've taken Mansour, I've slipped outside the lines. I'm not saying I'm special or that worse things haven't happened to better people. I'm not and they have. It's just that I know myself, or rather that I *don't* know myself anymore. Something has slipped, Henry. If you told me that all I had to do to free Mansour was pick up a knife and stab Uncle Nemec in the eye, I'd do it. Without hesitation. I'd do it."

And listening to these words, I know very suddenly that Selma is gone, that we won't be able to help her. She is lost to us. I can feel it in my chest, my throat, in a tingling in my fingertips. It's only intuition perhaps, but so powerful as to make itself physically felt. Have I known this all along? Isn't this feeling the one I had in the limousine on the way to Stephanie's birthday party when she first announced that Selma was coming—and bringing her troubles with her? But then in this same moment, I have a vision of myself in that college theater watching over and over the great French actor Gérard Depardieu playing the role of Cyrano de Bergerac and saying to his love, Roxane, even as he's dying, that the best fight is the one we know is in vain.

Selma is prepared to do anything to save her husband, even if that thing will destroy her in the process. This is what I believe she's said to me, here in this library with no one but the rows of books as witnesses. She feels that every choice available to her will result in calamity.

I finish rolling up my shirtsleeves and join Selma where she is standing by the window. There are mature trees, beds of tall grasses dotted with orange and yellow lilies all bordered by a low hedge. We are so close I can see where tears have left their salty tracks upon her cheeks.

There seems, finally, nothing left to say. I put my hand on her arm and she turns to me. Before I quite realize it my mouth is on hers and we are kissing, her tongue licking, tickling my lips.

Not now, but later, I will think that the only way to save somebody who has slipped beyond the lines is to wade out into the deep yourself and get them.

Nine

We wait through the whole of the afternoon and evening, through a long dinner of grilled steak and asparagus, through two bottles of red wine, before we kiss again, finally begging off by claiming to Uncle Nemec that we want to get an early start in the library. When we climb the stairs, Selma takes my hand and leads us down the dim hallway. My room is lit by the soft glow of a green-shaded reading lamp. I shake my head and keep whispering, "*Fuck, fuck, fuck,*" under my breath.

"Are you talking to yourself back there?"

"Maybe," I say. "No. Not really."

When we close the door behind us, Selma stands in the middle of the room and looks at me. There is a bemused half-smile on her face and her teeth are shockingly white in the dim light.

"I suddenly feel very foolish," I say. She doesn't reply. I watch her walk to the bedside table where Nemec has arranged a carafe of water. She pours a glass and takes a sip. The bed has been turned down and a chocolate left on the pillow like we are staying at a hotel.

"I'm so thirsty," she says.

"It was a lot of wine."

Selma had changed for dinner. The dress is pale green with thin straps that show off her dark shoulders. She hands me the glass and gathers her hair into a ponytail before letting it fall.

"Are you tired?" I say and take a sip of water.

"I'm sure I couldn't sleep." I pass the glass to her and watch as she traces a finger along the rim, shrugs her shoulders and smiles. Then she turns off the light.

For several moments we stand there, facing each other in the dark. When we can see again, Selma takes my hand and kisses it. Her lips are full and soft and cool. And when she grabs hold of me by the collar and kisses my mouth, her tongue is cool, too, and a little sour-tasting from the wine.

There is an unfamiliar scent in the air, Selma, and for a little while I let it disorient me. I think briefly of everything that I should not: of Mansour sitting in his prison, of Stephanie trusting me so completely with her friend, even of Selma's warning to me all those years ago, saying that I would pay a price for just such a night as this. But then Selma's hands are pulling at my belt, and just a moment later, I am watching her step out of her pretty green dress. Standing almost naked in front of each other, our noses touching, feeling Selma smile even in the dark, I push these other things away. I put my hands into her hair and let its silkiness fill the spaces between my fingers. Then I kiss her and quietly, between each kiss, whisper her name: *Selma.*

A car from the road brings light rolling in waves across the bedroom walls, and it is in these moments that we see the shape of our bodies together. We find our way to the bed. She says to me, her breath warm against my ear, "You've been wanting this." I slide her panties down to below her knees, then use my foot to push them away entirely, something white with frilly pink lace along the edges. I gather her to me so that our bodies press together, kiss her mouth again and again, then her neck. I pause there, the tiniest portion of her ear caught gently between my teeth, and breathe.

Heavy footsteps creak across the floor above us, Nemec maybe, imagining Selma and me together. But that is the last distraction as Selma's tongue slips into my mouth, tracing delicate little flickers along my lips. This is what I've wanted, isn't it? I've been a good person, do little harm in this world. This is my thought as I put my palm on Selma's stomach. I remember suddenly the last time I've had sex, Stephanie's birthday, with her rules, her steady pleasures—no matter how kind—and realize that Selma *is* what I have wanted.

I move both of my hands slowly up Selma's body until I find

hers and let our fingers lace playfully together, her hips pushing insistently against me; I want to drown, drown, drown, and forget myself—give it all over to some part of me that I was convinced I'd put aside, maybe forever. I think, inexplicably, of the look on Selma's face on Sunday afternoon when she first arrived, weeping into Stephanie's lap, the mascara running in dark rivers down her cheeks. She touches my face now, her hands rubbing against the rough stubble, her thumbs tracing the lines of my eyebrows.

"You *have* wanted this," she says, her voice catching on some unseen thing. Another wave of light rolls along the walls. Selma laughs—sweet pleasure and incredulity all at once. I laugh with her until kissing again, perhaps laughing still, we are both aware of my cock pressing impatiently against her thigh. She reaches down and grabs hold of me, her fingers tugging, and then guides me inside her. The expression of surprise on her face makes me look at her more closely: the parted mouth, her closed eyes, brow furrowed in concentration. In another moment I press deeper, resting my right hand at the base of her throat.

———

I wake to Selma's hair tickling across my chest. She is still asleep, her breathing deep and regular. For a moment I watch her back rise and fall. In the moonlight of the room with our bodies loosely tangled together under the covers, I feel peaceful. The movement that woke me must have been the smallest repositioning. The room is filled with our breath, with the scent of what we've done together. A clock at the bedside reads 3:12. Beside the clock is Virginia Woolf's *Orlando*. First edition. Very fine. And soon to be listed in the collection of one Thien Diep. As quietly as I can, gently, gently, I pick up the book and raise it to my nose and inhale the past. It is like sipping a much-needed cigarette or drinking the final swallow of a good wine.

I feel . . . nothing. My mind has been wiped clean with a strong chemical. I think of Henry Miller's wife, June, saying that after she had made love to Anaïs Nin she felt innocent. Perhaps this is what she meant.

Selma raises her head and squints at me with the book. She says, "What are you doing to that book? Kissing it?"

"I'm smelling it," I say. "Here."

I place the cut edges of the book under her nose and watch her reaction. "Mmm. I love that smell."

Selma kisses the book and then my hand holding it. She looks at me with such feeling, her eyes alive with nighttime light.

"This was one of the best days of my life," she says.

God, please don't thank me.

"Thank you." When I don't say anything she smiles. "It was completely romantic, you know? The house, all those beautiful books, Uncle Nemec's dinner. He's a charming old rascal. And so are you."

"I wish I could say that I planned it. I think."

"Are you feeling guilty?"

"Not yet," I say. "You?"

Selma sighs. "Let's not talk about it."

"This is a kind of 'love the one you're with' thing, I suppose," I say, though it makes me a little sick to admit it.

"Hmm," Selma says. "Maybe it's more like that variable thing you were talking about. Take an action and watch what opens up."

"That was just talk, you know. A thing you say."

"No. You meant it, and I think you're right." She reaches up to touch my face, rubs her fingertips along the stubble of my beard, walks her fingers over the top of my nose, traces circles around my eyes.

This intimacy feels natural. It belongs to us. The moment we take our lives outside of this room, though, everything will change. She is my wife's friend. I am her friend's husband. She is deeply in love with her husband. I am deeply in love with my wife. And so how can it be explained? A kiss may be explained away as impulse: Selma's difficult situation, the romantic location of Nemec's home, even pheromones. This is psychology, this is chemistry.

But coming to this room, removing our clothes, discovering each other's bodies. We could have stopped ourselves at any point and chose not to.

I kiss the top of her head and Selma snuggles closer. "Let's stop talking," she says. "Please."

In another moment or two our conversation tapers off. And like children, we fall asleep again, Selma settled comfortably against me, a strand of her hair in my mouth.

After breakfast the next morning, Selma and I spend another four hours in the library. It is a rich collection. There is a first edition of Hesse's *Siddhartha* in German (it turns out not all of the books are in English after all), Ford's *The Good Soldier*, Capote's *Breakfast at Tiffany's*, Shaw's *The Young Lions*. Selma is an excellent assistant, quick and focused. We are ready to return to Prague by early afternoon. Georg will drive us into Brno to catch the train, and Marketa and Nemec—the whole family—are there to see us off.

Nemec shakes my hand as we stand beside the Mercedes, the engine already running. "I almost hate to ask so bluntly," he says, "but what do you think they're worth?"

"I've got some homework to do on a few of those titles. But roughly? $150,000."

"Well," Nemec says raising his eyebrows, that easy lasciviousness playing across his face.

"Your wife had good taste. Even the more contemporary titles from the seventies and early eighties are worth hundreds of dollars."

"Ah, my Paulina. A last gift, perhaps, even from the grave."

We shake hands again and I explain the process for disposing of the collection. Except, of course, for the *Orlando* that I have with me and will sell right away, which clearly pleases Nemec immensely. For half a second, I wonder how much of this money Anna will actually receive.

And so, again, before I'm ready, I find myself settling into the train to Prague with Selma beside me poring over our notes from Nemec's collection.

Am I happy? Nearly.

Then something chokes up from a deep place inside me, and I am desperate to spit it out. A furiously sudden frustration at . . . what? My wife? My work? My friends?

Even at Uncle Nemec and his leering demeanor. At anything messy and human, to which I am normally so forgiving. Because what I see when I look at Selma is a mess — one that I want to clear away with a reckless sweep of my arm like papers from a desktop. I'm not satisfied with being a night's comfort in a time of sadness; I want more, but can't see what more would look like. What should be done is a deescalation, a backing down, a careful but absolute untangling. When Selma and I smile at each other now it will be knowing smiles, bittersweet, enriched by nostalgia. But at the future place I'm inventing — a dinner party at Jeb and Margaret's in North Carolina hosted by the senator to celebrate Mansour's release — we will exchange that smile and then return to the lives that we've built and to the spouses that we have chosen to share them with. It won't matter how beautiful Selma is or how much I care for her or how powerful the taste of her remains in my mouth. Because I'm the good guy, who's always a little surprised by his luck, a builder of this life that seems so big to me now, riding in a train with a lover across the Czech Republic. A builder, not a wrecker of lives.

It is in this way that I talk myself down. I reach out and take

Selma's hand and we smile. Then she gives that hand a little squeeze and rests her head on my shoulder.

"What do you think will happen," I say quietly, "if we just never get off this train?"

Selma doesn't answer because such things are not really questions. I can almost see the words, like print on a page, hovering briefly in the air above our heads before growing thin and being taken up by the wind and blown east toward Brno.

As we're walking from the train station with our overnight bags, we finally, out of necessity, begin to talk about what we'll do when we walk through the door to the apartment and are confronted with the fact of my wife.

"We only have a couple more blocks," I say.

Selma stops. She has a fist on her hip. "I know."

"Well? What should we do?"

She thinks for a moment and then sighs. Already it's a sound I'm getting used to. A little vision opens up briefly before me and I see, quite suddenly, part of what it might mean to be married to this woman.

"Let's do nothing for a little while," she says.

"Just pretend it didn't happen?"

"For now," she says. "I want to see what things feel like."

"What they *feel* like?"

"Yes."

And just like that, everything that had been graceful and

easy—beautiful, I don't think it wrong to say—feels awkward and absolutely fake, like a scene from one of the paperback romances my grandmother used to read. It is a story whose believability comes only from cliché, from its easy adherence to a formula we've all seen played out a million times.

"Okay," I say, "we'll see what things feel like."

"I think that's best."

Of course Stephanie is there when we walk in. She's been expecting us. Is anxious to see us. She's been exercising to pass the time. Yoga. Her cheeks are very prettily flushed and her eyes are wide and clear and glad at the sight of us. I feel an immediate urge to die of shame. It's a feeling akin to being caught masturbating in the back of seventh-grade science class. Awful.

"Oh, my God," she says. "You're finally back and I'm finally free. All the important people have packed up their little diplomatic cases and flown off to wherever they belong—not Prague!" She hugs and kisses us both. "Has he been taking good care of you, Selma?"

"Henry has been absolutely wonderful."

"Are you learning the book business? How did it go?"

Here is my wife. Excited to see her husband and to spend time with her friend. She doesn't have an inkling.

"Nemec has a beautiful collection. Anna should make a very nice sum. And we found something for Thien Diep."

"I saw it first," Selma says.

"Selma saw it first. An *Orlando*. First edition."

"Is that good?" Stephanie says, pretending ignorance. Who knows why? For the sake of conversation? To let Selma have a little moment in the sun?

"It's awesome. Henry says it's perfect for this Vietnamese woman's collection. And guess how much it's worth," Selma says.

Stephanie shakes her head and smiles. "Twenty thousand dollars."

"Well, that's the high end," I say. For some reason it seems incredibly important not to exaggerate.

"Let's go down to the Franz Kafka and have a drink to celebrate," Stephanie says. "You know, I can't believe she's been here this long and we haven't taken her."

"It's true," I say.

"Selma, we practically live there."

When Stephanie bounces back to our bedroom to change for the bar, Selma and I exchange a look. Well, Selma, I think, how do *things* feel?

It's powerful, the full light of my wife's attention. Stephanie takes a quick shower and puts on a lavender sundress. She doesn't dry her hair but only combs it out so that the straps of the dress become dark. She looks seventeen. When we go down to the Franz Kafka everyone, it seems, stops what they're doing to look at these two lovely women walking together arm in arm, giggling. Probably Stephanie feels bad about throwing her friend into my care, and now suddenly, as she said, she's free. To hell with missile defense systems. Goddamn and fuck all politics—at least for tonight.

Selma, it turns out, is quite good at pretending that she did not spend last night in my bed. At first, I'm not so talented. I'm too quiet. Listening. Watching. But of course they don't even notice me, so happy is Stephanie to spend time with her friend. After a while, my guilt just seems silly. We drink, we talk about books. Selma tells hilarious stories about Uncle Nemec, about how the dirty old man did everything he could short of pinching her bottom, which leads to shrieks and howls of delight from them both and the undivided attention of the bar. It strikes me then that Selma's not really putting on an act. I think of Fitzgerald's line about intelligence and the ability to hold opposing ideas in the mind at the same time, and realize that part of Selma can love her friend with all her heart while at the same time feel guilty about fucking me. Perhaps even now be thinking about how she'll arrange to be with me again. What would it be like to be the willing victim of a beautiful woman's plans? Not to chase, but to be ensnared? The idea excites me so much that I have to take a long drink of my beer and look for several minutes out into the mundane traffic of the street.

By the end of our meal we're each on to our third Pilsner. It has been a good evening after all: friends gathered around a table, food and drink, lively conversation, an antidote against everything in our lives that exists outside the café's walls. There are reminiscences from Coventry Drive. There are even moments of silent possibility as we gaze out at Prague. Again, but differently than before, I think about what it would be like to die. This moment.

When our dinner dishes are cleared away the waitress—I

love her, she's so perpetually sullen—brings coffee. Just before we settle in to drink it, Stephanie excuses herself to use the restroom, which is in the basement at the bottom of a long spiral staircase. As soon as Stephanie is out of sight, Selma takes my hand under the table and smiles.

"Henry," she says.

It's not a question. Just my name said in such a way as to describe love. "The evening is beautiful," I say.

"And you're happy, too?"

"This moment I am."

"Now you know what it's like to be me."

I don't say anything. Just nod my head. I'm smiling.

"Now maybe you know."

I look at her and think that she is perfect. Lovely, yes, but a woman whose mind is rich and teasing, who has made love to me so wonderfully. Could we actually walk away into some life together?

I lean in close to her, so close that my lips are touching her ear, my breath hot against her skin, and whisper her name.

"Oh, my God," Stephanie says when she returns. "You guys haven't even touched your coffee. Don't wait for me."

We have apple torte and then order a second round of coffees with shots of Kahlúa. Eventually the effect of so much travel and alcohol comes upon Selma and me. I pay the bill and leave the sullen waitress a generous tip. When we're back in the apartment, Selma says that she's going to bed. She wants to read *Possession* and fall asleep, she says, dreaming of star-crossed loves. Stephanie looks at me, but I just shrug my shoulders.

And then very soon, I find myself slipping under the covers beside my wife. My sexuality is utterly transformed. I have the chastity of a Catholic novitiate. Mercifully, Stephanie wants only to talk.

"She had a great time in Brno," Stephanie says. "What did you do to her?"

"It was no big deal. She got to travel with a friend."

"I wish I could have been there, too."

"Me, too," I say.

"Still," Stephanie says, "she's not herself. We've maybe put a really good bandage on it, but the hurt is still there."

This is the moment, I think. And this is what I should do. I should let my wife's words linger there between us, and in the moment that takes, I should think of Selma—savor the idea of what we've done together like lingering over the last page of a favorite novel, and then I should tell Stephanie . . . what? That her friend is still breaking down at random moments, so much so, in fact, that she tried to seduce me. Let her know that it's gone that far (but no further). Reclaim my place, where everyone already thinks I am, with the good guys, the people who are out to help Selma in this horrible time. That revelation would at least get Selma out of Prague and away from me. Selma would no doubt be sent somewhere—not back to New Jersey—probably to her family in Yemen. A stronger medicine. There'd be a real inter-vention then—or at least that's what we'd hope for.

I say, "That's what you do with hurts, isn't it? Bandage them up and wait for time to do its work?"

So no confession. I won't unmake what's happened. No

cautious path back to safety. I have spun a fantasy around us, Selma and me, not Romeo and Juliet, for God's sake, and not quite Dick and Nicole Diver, but something indelible from the pages of a book. And maybe that's it: I'd like to once more in my life feel like I'm living a story worthy of pages of literature rather than simply selling other people's stories—no matter how exquisitely made—for surprising sums of money. My tidy little shop in this fashionable city, manned, as it were, by a militantly gay assistant (forgive me, Morgan); it is a life that is relatively interesting when compared to the lives of accountants and lawyers and proctologists, but what is it really? The pleasure of putting a book in a customer's hand, like that little boy with his very nice edition of *The Hobbit*, who I imagine will now begin in earnest the development of his own inner life, the secret one where adventure is actually possible, unlike our shabby realities. Selma, though. Well. Here is a woman who has been touched by history: an Arab woman, a Muslim, living in the West, her husband arrested by a great power and pushed by neglect to the brink of death, while she travels the world turning over every possible stone to free him and save his life. To touch that life. It seems breathtaking, and I am drawn to her, to it, not against my will but like a sprinter with the wind at his back. Making love to such a woman is not just to fuck a body, of which there are millions, but to enter a life of such poignant complexity as to plunge yourself into an open electrical current. Or am I mad? I must be mad.

"You're right, I guess," Stephanie says. "I know that's right."

"We can only wait and see."

Stephanie turns out the light and we settle in together, the old routine. The stale smell of our hair and sweat on the pillowcases, the weight of my wife's body, which I know by heart as she settles into the mattress. In the quiet we are probably thinking about the same thing: Selma. But I envy Stephanie (almost) the purity of her thoughts, the innocence and friendship that her hopes for Selma take. Maybe now, in the dark, I could tell her what's happened, could also tell her what Selma wants her to do?

"Good night, sweetheart," she says.

"Sleep tight, darling."

I wake to Stephanie having a nightmare. Her dark dreams, whatever they may be, so often rise to the surface of her consciousness and result in a physical response: speaking, crying, whimpering, an almost feral twist, spasm, and jerk of her body. She's so close to being awake that all I need do is place the palm of my hand on her forehead and whisper her name, and she will awaken for a moment. She opens her eyes and looks at me, then she smiles.

"I was dreaming," she says.

"I know," I reply. And half a moment later her eyes are closed and she's sleeping peacefully again. I, however, as so often happens, am wide awake. I change positions a few times, turn over my pillow, bring one leg out from under the covers, but it's no use. I'll have to get up.

I pass by the door to Selma's room and imagine that I can feel the heat of her body lying in the bed. I think to make a noise, something like walking into the corner of the coffee table or dropping two ice cubes in a glass—a noise that will draw Selma out of her sleep and into the dark living room. Is it wrong to want to sit with her on the couch, shoulder to shoulder, as we did the night before our trip to Brno and drink in the scent of her hair? I pour myself a glass of water and sit there alone sipping at it, hoping that my presence will draw her to me. I shake my head. God. Out the window is Prague.

There's my street, Široká ulice, in its nighttime quiet. I retrace my insomniac walk from the night of Stephanie's birthday. The statue of Kafka, the Jewish Cemetery, Paris Avenue, the river. There is a gentle breeze coming in the window, cooling my skin, clearing the hair away from my forehead. A dog with his head out a car window.

So much to lose.

I back away from the window and drink the rest of my water in one long swallow. Selma has not come out.

Two closed bedroom doors. One I don't want to enter, the other I may not. The apartment is shrunken like a doll's house, and I turn in three directions before flinging myself onto the couch. One arm over my eyes.

Fuck.

If Stephanie were to come out now and try to bring me back to bed, what would I say? Something lame about needing air. A nightmare claustrophobia. Her own sleep is so often turbulent and disturbed that she would never question me. Only be surprised a little. Say something cute about how nightmares must be catching and hold her hand out to me.

But no one comes for me. For some time I try to sleep here on the couch. Dozing off. Twenty blissful minutes and then I'm awake thinking of Stephanie, as if those minutes away had never existed. Surely it will only be a matter of time before she sees that I love her friend. I feel the evidence of it glowing off my body like radiation. My wife is not so blind.

And then a thought. A game I used to play as a child, an only child living in a small place, yearning for friendship and a bigger world. At night after my mother had turned out the light and I'd said my prayers, I closed my eyes and envisioned an observatory on the top of a mountain surrounded by pines.

Inside there was a high gallery encircling a mammoth telescope from which I'd observe the universe, star by star, making minute (though largely incomprehensible) computations, and waiting more patiently than anyone might credit to make a discovery that would change everything. I had a very clear picture of the view from that telescope: the vast blackness of the sky, the silver-white light of a star, or the dusty wastes of the moon. To gaze so far always took my feelings, whatever they might have been, and stretched them thin, so that what I was left with was a calm nothingness. It was what I needed now, and it felt like an inspiration to have thought of this game on tonight of all nights, when a child's wisdom seemed as good as any other and the idea of my feelings—so savagely confused—stretched to a nondescript thinness would be nothing short of a blessing.

What would it be like to travel the solar system the way a tourist travels ten miles of track on a steam engine? The scenic view of Mars, Jupiter, and on your left, folks, Neptune. Is outer

space silent? Or is there a calming white noise, a background
of wind still blowing round and round since the Bang? That's
what I would hope for: a gentle hum to accompany my view.

And with that I am gone. Asleep finally with nothing but my
dreams to cover me until morning.

———

"Selma!" This is Stephanie's voice shouting through the apartment. Selma is gone. Her little suitcase is missing and *Possession*
is centered neatly on her pillow.

Stephanie stomps around from room to room calling her
name, but I know she's not here. "She just left? In the middle of
the night?" She is incredulous.

My wife finally stops thundering around the apartment and
stands in the middle of the living room with her hands on her
hips. I'm in the study beside the pullout bed and fingering the
corner of the book.

"See if she left a note," Stephanie says.

I pick up the book and fan its pages. Nothing. "No," I say.
"She's just gone."

When I finally fell asleep I must have been so exhausted I
didn't hear her roll by with a suitcase. Didn't hear the door
close.

After a moment, Stephanie and I simply stare at each other,
trying to decide if there's anything to be done.

"Call her cell phone," I say.

She does, but of course no one answers.

"Why did she leave?" Despite an effort, Stephanie's eyes begin to tear up. I know what's going through her mind. She is free finally, out from under the yoke of work, and ready to spend time with Selma, to do her part, and now she's been cheated out of the chance.

"Maybe it's nothing bad," I say. "Or nothing so bad. She might be doing something. Having a private adventure. Maybe it was something she didn't want to have to explain."

"Is that really what you think?"

"No. But it's possible."

So this is Selma's decision: simply slip away in the night. Not a word, not a gesture, not an explanation.

I feel stricken. Like someone has taken a divot out of my chest with a blunt object. I want so much to hear her singing in the shower again. Those Arabic love songs.

Stephanie says, "You didn't hear her leave?" She's pointing at the couch where I had been sleeping.

"No. I was totally out."

"What could have happened?" she says. I shake my head.

Stephanie goes to the window and looks out, much as I did the night before. It strikes me that Selma might have already been gone and that it was already only a phantom I was hoping would come and find me. Stephanie crosses her arms over her breasts and lets her head rest against the glass. She has failed her friend, that's what she thinks. And maybe worse, she will have to call her friends, maybe even Selma's family, and report the failure in all its detail.

"I just can't understand what went wrong."

Once again a broad door conveniently labeled TRUTH swings open before me. All I have to do is walk through it. I should have faith in my wife; we've been married a long time. Surely, we could not be so easily unmade. She must see that her friend is unhinged, that her husband has been a fool, and that, to some degree, so has she. No one gets to be innocent in this.

I walk up behind her and slide my arms around her waist and hold her there. We've both been abandoned. In a perverse sort of way it makes sense to be comforting each other. It is, besides, what married couples do. Or can do, if they choose to.

"We'll hear from her again," I say. "And probably soon. We just have to wait."

"Oh, God, I'm so bad at waiting. You know that."

"I do."

In a little while it's decided that I should go to the Hades. I have work to do, but more importantly it occurs to us both that Selma might show up there.

I think I know better.

Yet in a moment we begin to execute this plan: taking showers, getting dressed, going down to the Kafka for coffee. Our cell phones always in easy reach.

Ten

All the world might go mad, but the Hades is the same as ever: quiet, a little dusty, air-conditioned to a livable temperature against the Prague summer heat. Morgan is there like a swaggering Charon awaiting his first fare of the day. I'm not in the shop for ten seconds before I have the *Orlando* out of my briefcase and lying on the counter between us for inspection. It is not a book that the Woolfs hand-printed themselves on their home press but one that was sent out to commercial printers. Still, it has the aura of something precious uncovered from the ashes of Pompeii. The story of an English nobleman of always somewhat androgynous character who is transformed over three centuries of history into a car-driving, child-bearing modern woman of the 1920s. A transformation, that is, in the hands of Woolf's language, both inexplicable and inevitable. If Woolf's diaries and letters are to be believed (for when does a fiction writer ever stop creating?), she thought of it as a lark, an entertainment, serious perhaps in its way, but only really meant for fun and to woo her love, Vita Sackville-West, who was, let's call it, inconstant. It is not a book that I love, but I do remember it fondly as the first book of VW's that I could actually read and understand—the language being more accessible to my twenty-year-old mind than that of *Jacob's Room* or *Mrs. Dalloway.* And I think Woolf was right. *Orlando* is not a great book. But for readers whose lives are sympathetic with its theme, it is a very important text, a big, blockbuster Hollywood movie moment in Woolf's career of Academy Awards for Best Supporting Actress. This book is sexy, flamboyant. Thien Diep will be thrilled.

For Morgan and me, it is a nice distraction. And, of course, it's difficult not to think about the money. Though today, of all days, my cut isn't that much of a draw, and I find myself faking it a bit to match Morgan's enthusiasm. What I need is . . . I need to see Selma.

I take the *Orlando* back to my office and boot up the computer. Thien Diep will have to be called. My buyer for the Fitzgerald from San Sebastian. There are things to do. Absolutely. This should be an exciting day for the Hades. A banner day. A day to break out the champagne.

Come find me, Selma.

"You have reached Thien Diep. I am not available to come to the phone right now, but you if leave your name and number I will return your call at my earliest convenience." *Beep.*

All right, then. A day of missed connections.

"Hey, Thien! It's Henry Marten. Sorry I couldn't call you yesterday as we'd discussed, but listen: I've got something for you. I almost don't want to tell you what it is, but since I've made you wait a day longer than promised, I suppose I must. Are you sitting down, Thien? Okay? It's an *Orlando.* Thien, this book is in perfect condition. Nothing will mar your enjoyment of this book. Truly. Give me a call back when you get this and we'll work out the details. Hope you're as excited as I am. Talk to you soon!"

That wasn't so bad. Very nearly genuine. Okay, good.

Still, I can't bring myself to call Bechtsold about his plans to visit the Fitzgerald. From my briefcase I take out a second book. The copy of *Possession* that I gave to Selma and which she abandoned on her pillow as she fled the apartment. I feel pathetic, handling the book only to touch what she has touched. I put the pages of the book to my nose hoping not for the telltale scent of vanilla as the pages slowly break down, but somehow of Selma. I open the cover and, with my thumb, slowly fan the pages.

Just over a third of the way, the text is marked in pencil. Half a paragraph underlined in a steady hand. It is one of the letters that Christabel LaMotte has written to Randolph Henry Ash when she has decided they cannot be together.

Oh Sir—things flicker and shift, they are indeed all spangle and sparks and flashes. I have sat by my fireside all this long evening—on my safe stool—turning my burning cheeks towards the Aspirations of the flame and the caving-in, *the ruddy mutter, the* crumbling *of the consumed coals to—to where am I leading myself—to* lifeless dust—*Sir.*

I feel tears in my eyes. Hot and a little shameful. To cry over lines that may or may not have even been read by Selma let alone noted. And yet. I laugh at myself for crying. I must be tired, tired and played out.

Of course, Morgan chooses this moment to breeze into the office. Poor man. He stops short as soon as he sees my face.

"What's happened?" he says. His voice is all business and filled with genuine concern.

"Selma's gone," I say and tell him the whole story. All of it.

"Son of a bitch," he says, shaking his head and smiling. "I didn't know you had it in you."

"I've fucked this up, Morgan."

His look is a little contemptuous. "Well, you certainly had a hand in the pot, but it's pure egotism to take all the credit."

"Everyone knew she was on the edge. Our job was to bring her back. If anything, I pushed her over the edge."

"A little defenestration, eh?"

"Don't joke."

"Seriously then? Just because she's left your house doesn't mean that something bad has happened. Probably she realized that staying there was too awkward. You probably ought to be thanking her for saving your marriage."

"You think she's all right?"

"Well. Perhaps only marginally worse than when you found her."

"Thanks," I say, meaning "Fuck you."

"Besides, it sounds like she did an awesome job with Nemec. And that's what's important—you might need all the money you can get."

"For what?"

"The divorce."

I throw the stapler from my desk at his head, but he ducks out of the way easily and the cheap plastic splinters into pieces when it smashes against the wall. Morgan's laughter carries back from the front of the shop.

As I kneel down to clean up the broken stapler, I begin to laugh, too—quietly. I would never give Morgan the satisfaction. Despite being an asshole, he's lightened my mood. No doubt what he'd intended.

I'm throwing the stapler in the trash when my cell phone rings. Please God, let it be her.

"Hello."

"Henry?"

"Selma, where are you?"

"I'm at a hotel."

"Which hotel?"

"I'd rather not say."

At least she's not dead. Thank God. "What are you doing?" I say.

"I just had to leave, you know?"

This is where I say that she's scared me to death, that I was sure something horrible had happened to her, that I love her and can't live without her. Though I'm not sure how true any of those things are. Some of them feel true.

What I say instead is, "No, I don't know. Let's talk about this."

"Okay, but not on the phone. I hate the phone."

"You know you've scared the shit out of Stephanie."

"Where should we meet?" she says. Her voice is cold, like someone transacting an unpleasant business in which they are fully aware they hold all the cards. Suddenly I can't think of a single place in all of Prague.

"Meet me at the castle," she says finally. "I want to see the changing of the guard."

Bizarre, but why not. She can see Kafka's house while she's at it.

"Okay. The guard will change at"—I look at my watch to see the time—"noon." The line goes dead.

"Selma, right?" This is Morgan calling in from the front where he's dusting the shelves.

"Right."

I sit back in my chair and breathe. The *Possession* lies there on the desk and I place my palm on the cover. The love story between Randolph Henry Ash and Christabel LaMotte was tragic. What kept them apart? Circumstance, certainly. Misunderstanding. It was crushing. But their love also sustained them for decades, took up residence in their day-to-day lives and powered his greatest poetry. And, of course, their love set in motion a set of circumstances that showed future generations how to love. The book argues that as an affair of the heart, their relationship was a resounding success. All true, perhaps, but I am not comforted.

Selma will tell me that in the cold light of day what we did together in Brno has infected her with a cancerous guilt. She will paint pictures of her jailed husband and of her wronged friend. She will say that it is a beautiful memory. She will not, for example, suggest the renting of a flat in Istanbul, from the balcony of which we can watch the sunlight play along the waters of the Bosphorus. Though what if she did say that? Or what if I did and she were to accept?

I stand in the doorway of the office and look out into the front of the store. The tidy space, its rows and rows of books, its signature scent, my friend's practiced movements as he makes his way from one small task to the other. And outside? Prague. And all that the city has come to mean to me. Would it be possible to walk away? I close my eyes and feel Selma's body beneath my hands. It's not hard to envision us on that balcony overlooking the Bosphorous, sitting at a small table, and eating omelets and drinking mimosas. It's an unsettling feeling to know that you will lose no matter which choice is made.

This is the moment that the bell over the door tolls and Bechtsold walks in. He is small and wiry with bright, merry eyes and perpetually dressed in white. He reminds me a little bit of a Swiss Tom Wolfe. This morning he smiles sheepishly and spreads his arms wide to beg for our indulgence.

"I couldn't wait even another moment for your call," he says. "Tell me that you still have it."

He means, of course, the Fitzgerald. Morgan and I step forward to shake his hand and smile our welcomes.

"We would never sell a book like this out from under you," I say.

"Am I that good of a client? Perhaps that's a reputation I don't particularly want to have."

"Don't worry," Morgan says. "We'll tell everyone that you're surly and difficult and drive a hard bargain."

"Is the book everything you've suggested?" he says, ignoring Morgan.

"Why don't you have a look for yourself?"

Bechtsold can't resist a broad smile. He is a serious collector, a man for whom books mean more than food or drink, more than most people, more, probably, than love. He is engaged heart and soul. I imagine him a little bit like a child with his superhero action figures. Handling them each day, changing their poses, engaging them in imaginary confrontations. So it must be with his books. A whole imaginary world created for himself, protecting him from God knows what. Were he less wealthy, he'd probably be me, running his own bookshop where he could at least be the middleman. No wonder I like him so well.

"Morgan," I say, "will you bring it out?"

"This is the best moment, isn't it, Henry?"

"It is, it is. I've felt privileged to keep it in my possession even this long. You'll see."

"Ach, you know how to play with a man's feelings. I might have a coronary."

"Well, we can't have that. The book's total shit," I say. "Worthless. A third printing with baby vomit sticking the pages together." We laugh. Peter's a good sport.

"May I offer you a drink? Coffee, tea, something stronger?"

"No, no."

Morgan lays the Fitzgerald on the counter in front of him. It's a beautiful reaction. Peter turns slightly and raises himself momentarily onto the toes of his right foot. He brings two fingers to his mouth, like a bon vivant preparing to blow a lady a kiss, before exhaling audibly.

He hasn't even touched the book yet when he says, "Imagine it, Henry. Fitzgerald himself touched this book. Before *Gatsby*. Before Zelda went insane. On the climb up the long hill of his New York debaucheries. Before he'd escaped to Paris and met Hemingway. Oh my, just think."

"You're the reason I love this business, Peter." I clap him on the back. "Take your time with it. If you have any questions just ask Morgan. I absolutely must step out for a few moments."

Morgan raises his eyebrows, confused, and then all at once understands. "Carpe diem," he says, and returns his full attention to Peter.

I pop back into the office and grab *Possession* off the desk. Stop. Open the file cabinet and take a long pull of Johnnie Walker Black. Pick up the book again and I'm out the door without looking anyone in the eye.

It is not a long walk from the Hades to the castle, but a steep one that is hot and baked in sunlight. At close to noon, there are multitudes crowding the pathway. I will be sweating by the time I reach the top of the hill and the tourist entrance and so have set out early in order to reach the top in time to find a shady spot under some stony rampart under which to cool off before I meet Selma for what could be, if things go badly, the last time. Each step forward is an anticipation, a feeling of pure excitement that (no longer a child, not yet old) I'm able to appreciate even while it's happening. Like a ten-year-old on a bike with the whole of a summer's day unfolding before me. Even if the day should end poorly, even violently, the important thing is to feel alive.

I am ten minutes early and, wiping my hairline dry, find a patch of shade. The guards are about fifty yards away, stoic, impassive, dressed in the powder-blue uniforms—clearly chosen for being some of the most handsome men in the Czech nation, they do a passable imitation of the British Beefeaters. It's a nice touch, I suppose. And tourists stand beside them to have their pictures taken.

And into this scene, graceful as ever, walks Selma wearing the same green dress from the night of our dinner with Nemec, the night she made love to me, her dark hair long and curling below her shoulders.

I walk up behind her as she's admiring the guards and touch her elbow. "Selma?"

"I knew you'd find me," she says. When she turns her smile is radiant.

I don't know what I expected. That she would somehow be transformed. If anything, she's more beautiful than ever. The noonday sun has probably warmed her hair, which looks like black fire. I want to touch it.

I can't hide *Possession* and so use it as my first move. "You forgot your book."

"Not forgotten exactly." She does not reach out to take it.

"Okay," I say. "What's going on?"

"I couldn't stay."

"Could you elaborate on why not?" I say, walking us toward my spot of shade.

"Some places are good for you, some places aren't. Your apartment was very good for a while, now it is not."

"That sounds like a bad fortune cookie. Don't you think I deserve a little better than that?"

As soon as this last line is out of my mouth, I hate it. I want to swallow it back like a spoonful of bitter medicine and never let it see the light of day. It sounds whiny and defensive. It is the opposite of declaring my love gracefully and letting the chips fall where they may.

"Probably," she says.

Then for a moment there is nothing to say. No momentum to carry us forward together. I'm not even quite sure what it is I want. I am still torn somewhere between Istanbul fantasies and tucking Selma back into the fold so that Stephanie will feel less bad about herself. Because it's clear that if Selma simply disappears, my wife will forever blame herself. It occurs to me that I have absolutely no control over the situation.

"Have you asked her?" Selma is looking at the castle, at the guards, at the people passing by—everywhere but at me.

"No. I haven't asked her yet."

"But you will ask her?"

"Your disappearing pushed all that out of my mind."

"Please ask her. You *need* to ask her."

"Selma," I say, taking her hand.

She sighs. It is not some long and dramatic exhalation but only a quick noise that her normal poise couldn't prevent. As soon as it's over, she offers me a testy little smile.

She says, "You're not listening. I need you to focus on what I'm telling you." Whatever breeze had been blowing seems to suddenly cease, and all I can feel is the noonday sun baking the top of my head and a line of sweat rolling down my back. I look over at the guards, at their stoic expressions made almost poignant by the antics of the crowd roiling around them. Almost poignant, if it weren't just theater. A play. A game.

"So it wasn't love then?"

For a moment I think Selma will choose not to answer. But then something seems to occur to her. "It was love," she says, "just not for you."

So this is what I'm meant to understand: Convince your wife to influence her friend at the embassy to help Mansour, and that night in Brno stays safely between us. For you, *me*, it can remain a lovely moment, a sweet memory. An exotic fantasy fulfilled. Otherwise, it will surely mean the end of your marriage.

It seems that what I wanted was to be a figure of note, a rook or knight, instead of merely a pawn. I wanted my life to feel as if it could walk off the pages of a great novel, something that kids would read about in school and from which some aphoristic lesson could be imparted: grace under pressure, the death of the American dream, something sturdy and knowable about love. Up until this moment, I believed that was possible.

"I'll do whatever I can to help you, Selma."

"Good boy."

"How do you envision this playing out?"

"You'll leave here and go visit Stephanie at the embassy. You'll tell her what I need her to do for Mansour. In a perfect world, she'll snap up the chance to do the right thing. If the right thing isn't immediately obvious to her, you'll exert your husbandly influence."

"Okay. And if she agrees?"

"Then I'll be waiting in my hotel for a call from Mr. Albert Jones, Diplomat, United States Embassy, Czech Republic."

Do the right thing. Exert my husbandly influence. There's not a shred of genuine feeling for me in all of this plan. There never was. The idea of renting a flat in Istanbul, of eating a postcoital brunch on the balcony overlooking the Bosphorus, never even crossed her mind.

All of it to save her husband. I don't know whether to admire Selma Al-Khateeb or despise her.

"All right," I say, "let's see what we can do."

"You promise?"

I nod. "Just find a way to work things out with Stephanie. She doesn't deserve any of this."

Selma takes my hand and kisses me on the cheek. Very quietly she says, "It turns out this is a war, Henry. Everyone must choose a side."

Is it possible for malice and kindness to live together in one gesture, one sentence?

"Stephanie will know what to do," I say. And I suddenly realize that I believe this.

"Talk to her," Selma says.

Now I am faced with the fact that it's time to leave. Probably forever.

The crowd stirs all around us at the changing of the guard. The sun is a fireball hovering overhead. The air is laced with the smell of grilled meat.

"Go now," she says. "Go talk to her."

We begin to drift apart, and then as if at a signal, Selma turns on her heel and disappears into a wall of people. The crowd seems to open to accept her and then closes again, and she is gone.

My worst self will not be fed. I will not, it seems, pyrotechnically destroy my marriage, a fifteen-year friendship. I will not mine my vast book collection for language to help justify a grand passion, I will not immerse my life into an East/West love that will test the zeitgeist. I will instead have to find a way down from this fairy-tale castle and back into the Hades, into the air-conditioned cool commerce, into the business of selling other people's stories.

Despite what I have said to Selma, I do not immediately go to the embassy. Instead, I walk back down the hill to the Hades where I imagine myself able to think whatever best thoughts I am capable of within its calm, air-conditioned walls. When I arrive, however, Bechtsold and Morgan are standing outside on the pavement smoking cigars together.

"You've returned just in time for the celebration," Morgan says, removing the thick stogie from his mouth and dramatically blowing smoke in the air above his head.

I shake Bechtsold's hand and he gives me a cigar of my own from a leather case that he keeps tucked away inside a jacket pocket. Morgan will tell me later what price they agreed upon, but by his enthusiasm I trust he's done us proud. Besides, the Swiss did not come here to haggle, he came to possess the Fitzgerald.

"You've bought yourself a little slice of immortality," I say to him.

Bechtsold nods to me vigorously, his eyes a little wet with emotion, as he watches me cut the cigar and light up. It's a fine cigar, and I tell him so. He takes my arm and gives it a squeeze like we're old friends. While we're all chatting each other up in that chirpy language of self-congratulation, I think about the tidy profit I've just earned and the one just around the corner when I finalize the sale of the *Orlando* to Thien Diep. I'm thinking that for the Hades this is going to be a good year. Perhaps the best yet. My little enterprise is making itself into a success. Not enough to make me rich or even close, but successful enough to be written up every year in the *Prague*

Post, to be sought out by thoughtful tourists and grudgingly admired by the Czechs. I use it to convince myself that I am not miserable. Or that when one door closes another opens. Or any of the other silly things we say to ourselves when the great zeppelin of our lives feels like it has gone down in a fiery crash.

Inside the shop again, I do a very careful job of wrapping up the Fitzgerald, tucking the bill of sale safely between pages 15 and 16. I pretend to carefully inspect the check Bechtsold has written and earn myself a small chuckle. Soon we are all standing in the doorway shaking hands again and saying our good-byes. Morgan and I watch him walk down the street and around a corner before we go inside again.

"We should close up and go get ourselves the most exquisite lunch in the Czech Republic!" Morgan says.

I shake my head, say something glib about food not being my friend today, or something similar. He is disappointed, and I feel like shit saying no. It's not often that I let Morgan handle, alone, the negotiation of a big sale. Not even with a man as ready to spend his money as Bechtsold. Probably Morgan also wants to get a drink or two in me and pull out all the juicy details of Selma. Then follow it up with a long and, from his point of view, healthy advice session.

"But I'll tell you what," I say. "Why don't you take the rest of the afternoon off? Paid, of course. Besides, I owe you one from the other day."

I can tell that Morgan doesn't want to go. Neither of us really thinks of the Hades as work. Still, a free afternoon off in Prague, in summer, is not a thing one usually says no to.

"You can't think of any way to spend your time? No trysts of your own to pursue?"

This makes him smile. And why not? Begrudge no one their happiness.

"You're a true friend, Henry," he says. "But call me if things get dicey. I'll bring the cavalry to rescue you from the clutches of all these women."

"You're on speed dial," I say, and five minutes later I am alone.

When I think Morgan is safely away, I lock the door and place the CLOSED sign in the window. Then I turn up the classical music station we always have playing while we're open and pour myself a scotch. Not a single sound save the music, which is a gentle wash upon every surface in the room, especially upon the solitary figure of me. In the past, it has always been a great balm to be alone inside the Hades. The geometry of the books, the warmth of the wood, in daytime the luminous shafts of broken sun lighting the room like a happy childhood memory. I take a drink. Whatever I'm about to do, I don't want to blunder into it as I have with so much over the past week. There must be, from the safety of this place, a way to make a good decision. There must be. There must. Or so I think to myself as I pace the room, raising a cover or two on the front table and letting them gently fall closed.

Must.

It strikes me then that I have been wrong about something. My life, which I'd decided could only reach its most meaningful—worthy of literature—if I became Vronsky to Selma's Anna, has actually embroiled itself in something story worthy. My mistake was to envision myself as the protagonist of my own narrative when I am at best a foil to some greater actor.

What would I be like in the hands of my heroes? Kafka, Miller, Kundera. Those men were the makers of monsters. Twists of human flesh both political and psychological. Perhaps I will be found lying on the page, panting, a fetus with a cigar in his mouth. And a book, just out of reach.

Suddenly it is clear that whatever it is that I will do, it cannot be accomplished here, in this place. Quickly then, the music is off and the key turned in the lock. A moment to take in the blue afternoon sky, to breathe in the air of the city, and I am off.

———

The embassy of the United States of America. Richly engraved double doors, framed by a gray stone portico, on the top of which is the seal of my country. Above the portico is a long pole flying the Stars and Stripes, and above this, a heraldic crest of some moment in Czech history—maybe even the Hapsburgs. I'm sure I've been told more than once.

Since we've been in Prague, I have often visited the embassy for evening functions but rarely make an appearance during business hours. Stephanie's made it clear—she doesn't want me around. Nothing personal, but people in the embassy talk about spouses who flit in and out of the building as though it were the local Walmart. And so there's no doubt she knows it is something serious, something to do with Selma, when the receptionist calls her office to announce me.

"What is it?" she whispers as we hustle down the hall.

When we're in her office she shuts the door and gestures for me to sit in one of the chairs across from her desk.

"Did you hear from Selma?"

I nod. Across the room is a Louis XIV table that Stephanie uses as a sideboard. In the center are a Czech crystal carafe and four water glasses. On either side are black-and-white framed photographs—one of her father and one of our wedding day.

"Where is she?" she asks. "What's she doing? For God's sake, Henry, don't just sit there like you've been struck dumb."

"She's taken a room at the Hotel U Kočku."

"Why on earth would she want to do that?" Stephanie says. It's clear that she's worried, incredulous, but also totally out to sea. She has no idea that her husband has betrayed her with her friend, or that that friend has become someone she would hardly recognize.

I clear my throat and sit up just a little bit straighter. "Something is happening with Mansour," I say. "Or what I mean is, Selma's trying to make something happen."

"God, you should see your face, Henry. This is going to be bad, isn't it?" Stephanie is putting on a brave smile, a rueful one that seems to say *Here we go.*

I lean forward a bit in my chair and rest the palms of my hands on the polished top of her desk and try to decide how much I will tell her.

"Selma didn't just come to visit us *to get away from it all* for a while."

"Go on," she says, genuinely encouraging me. I'm having trouble—she can see that—but I have information she desperately wants to know.

"Has Selma ever mentioned the name Albert Jones to you?"

"Al? Why would she mention him? How would she even know him?'

"Remember the other day when you had to work late and I entertained Selma until you could get away? The night we eventually met up with Anthony and his friend?"

"Of course."

"That was the day she told me her plan," I say, and explain all about Albert Jones and how he's law school pals with Jacob Sprecher, who is handling Mansour's case. I recount everything she said about these men, and how Selma wants Stephanie to exert her influence—whatever that might mean—in order to get Sprecher to act on Mansour's behalf. I even tell her Selma's idea about the plan's simplicity—just the "pulling of a lever" in some quiet, sealed-off room deep in the bowels of governmental officialdom.

The phone rings and I watch Stephanie transform her face from shocked confusion to something more businesslike. She raises a finger for me to wait and picks up the phone.

"Stephanie Marten. Oh, hi. Listen, I'm with someone. May I call you right back? Good. I will. Okay. Talk to you in just a few minutes. Okay, thanks. Bye." She had been giving one of those little professional laughs, a polite chuckle, I guess, at that last "Okay, thanks," but now the chuckle has been strangled off.

"Why didn't she just ask me herself?"

"She didn't think you'd do it unless I persuaded you."

"Why not?"

"Selma doesn't believe that you'll compromise your professional integrity. I don't remember if that was the exact phrase she used but that was the gist of it."

"Well, she's right."

For a moment there doesn't seem to be anything to say. I let my gaze stray out the window at the sunshine, at a patch of blue sky. Another perfect summer day in Prague.

This is the moment when if I were to do as Selma has asked that I'd turn on some husbandly charm. All I say, however, is "What do you think we should do?"

Stephanie's face is as blank as I've ever seen it. Cream-colored construction paper from which all the markings have been carefully erased.

"What should *we* do?" she says.

"Yes."

I prepare myself for a sharp dressing down on the logistics of betrayal. All that I've withheld until this moment, all I've now said, what continues, perhaps, to be hidden. She would have every right to do so. Until this moment, she has thought that we were moving through this life together.

Instead, a single tear wells up in her left eye and I watch it spill down her cheek. And I realize that what she's feeling is not my betrayal but Selma's.

"She came here to manipulate us," I say.

"She did."

"Do you remember what you said to me about Selma? It was the night of your birthday. You said, I want her to be surrounded by people who believe in Mansour's innocence."

Stephanie wipes the tear away and nods.

"So then let's be those people. Would it have been better if Selma had just come begging for help? Yes. No one likes to be manipulated." An image of Selma's bare shoulder in the moonlight that has to be shaken away. "But would it really be so hard to talk to this Albert Jones? Tell me if I'm being naïve, but isn't that how things get done in your world?"

This earns me a snort of laughter and a half-smile. "You've been reading too many novels."

"Guilty," I say. "But seriously. Is there any harm in doing what she wants?" Stephanie holds up her hand—a signal for me to wait, to be silent. Whatever decision she makes, it will be a different one from mine. I am motivated by both the night spent in Brno and by a harsh return to a wholly different reality. But my feelings are framed by those two extremes, both of which represent only Selma, Selma, Selma. For Stephanie, her friend is only a single variable. The business of the government of the United States of America is another.

"Tell me again how Selma thinks this is going to work," she says.

"Okay, here's her thinking. One. Mansour is innocent. Two. It's only a matter of time before the FBI or the INS or whoever comes to that decision. Three. A word from a trustworthy insider can solve the whole business now. Something

Selma thinks is essential because she's convinced that Mansour is going to die in prison."

It is a powerful idea, the possibility—no matter how remote—that you hold someone's life in your hands.

Stephanie is shaking her head no, but no to what? "What is it?" I say.

"Has it struck you that maybe Mansour isn't innocent?"

Have I not just been thinking about spouses and their ability to surprise? How often in an established marriage does one spouse truly surprise the other? Or even entertain the possibility that surprise is possible? It's like walking into a room and seeing your wife sitting with great composure upon the couch—back straight, legs demurely crossed—and seeing her beating heart lying there on the cushion beside her. Stephanie's question bubbled up from a place wholly new to me.

"But I thought—" I begin.

"I know, I know," Stephanie says, waving my words away, "but think about what it would mean if he were being held legitimately."

"Do we think this?"

"Do you know, really know, one way or the other?"

"But Selma . . . "

" . . . would still love her husband regardless of his politics."

"What are you saying?"

"That privately I can love Mansour, too, regardless of his politics. But as a representative of the government of the United States? Imagine if I set Selma's plan in motion. Imagine that Mansour is released. Then imagine that he's not innocent."

"You would be implicated," I say.

"It would mean the end of my career, but more than that, it would be a decision that I'd have to live with for the rest of my life."

"And if he's innocent and dies in that dirty New Jersey prison?"

I think back to the Stephanie I fell in love with on Coventry Drive. Still a girl, really, with her coltish legs, like the photo I have of her on my own desk in the Hades. I remember the night that I met them all. All those beautiful, interesting women. Dangerous and mysterious-seeming to someone as inexperienced as me. And Selma, the best among them—or so they always thought. I try to imagine how that young Stephanie with her foreign-service-exam cram book would become this woman sitting at the desk across from me, faced with such an ugly decision. She should at least have all the facts.

And so I say, "There's something else you should know."

This is where, in a certain kind of movie, the camera would begin to move away from the characters. The shot would widen to take in the black-and-white photos on the sideboard, the flag's gentle undulations in the breeze outside, the rooftops of this thousand-year-old city, surviving as it has through time with its stretch of blue sky and sunshine.

I have wanted to be a character in a novel, someone significant, if not great, whose life could stand outside of time. What I realize is that I've embroiled myself in something much more dangerous. Real life has sharp edges that we normally do our best to avoid but on which I have very nearly impaled myself.

Outside the embassy doors Michael is sitting at a favorite table in the Globe and sharing a coffee with his wife. Selma is on the edge of her bed praying that the phone will ring. Anthony, if he's not trying to get one more fuck out of Belinda before she returns to New York, is back at the Senate building following the missile defense talks. And Morgan is standing at a bar telling Bloody Sunday stories, all of which are pure fiction, to pick up a young hipster with piercing blue eyes.

The same sun that burns the cobblestones in Prague is shining in through the windows of Milos Nemec's library. The room is empty, still and silent as a mausoleum, dust motes floating in the air untroubled by even Marketa's cloth.

That is where so much of our time lives, empty rooms where the seconds and minutes beat unnoticed. The real life, truly, when all of our hubris is set aside. A grave quietude that so few of us know how to embrace and that most of us fight against tooth and nail. Myself included.

And so here we are again, in this warmly decorated room in the U.S. embassy, a husband and wife sitting together revealing secrets and making decisions.

It is either a gift or a curse to sit in such a room and to be able to see it already as a memory. I am chilled by the way I feel time bend and pause, do a little bow. The feeling clears away a skein of cloud from my eyes and they are wide open, drinking in all the light, every subtle shift and movement. I've been a fool, it's true. But I'm not useless. My life isn't over. Not yet. This story, I find, does not have to neatly end here.

I reach out and touch my wife's hand.

She is striking, awash as she is in ambivalence. Her face has been refreshed, the message of her features transmitting again to those of us who know her private language. She is before me now just as she has always been. I should be grateful. I am.

"Will you call Selma?" I say.

Her voice, when she answers, is calm, even in tone, almost sweet. There is in it, if you know how to listen, a decision she's comfortable with. There may still be uncertainty, there may still be some as-yet-unlooked-for reckoning, but the main thing has been found.

"No," she says, "I think not."

Acknowledgments

I am grateful to many people who have been essential to the writing of this book. Especially to Glenn Kent and Morgan Marietta, who are the foundation of my life and who took me to Prague—this book is yours. To Robert Peluso for being my drinking buddy and my literary friend—though that might be redundant. To Jeb Feldman at the Unsmoke Artspace for giving me a place to write, because as Henry Miller says, "Onc can sleep almost anywhere, but one must have a place to write." To Steve Yarbrough and Stewart O'Nan for being so giving of their time and advice. To Jack Shoemaker at Counterpoint for taking a chance. To Valerie Borchardt for opening so many doors. And, as always, to the memory of Mark Perlman, who believed in me.

About the Author

Jeffrey Condran is the author of the story collection *A Fingerprint Repeated*. His work has been honored with several awards, including *The Missouri Review's* William Peden Prize and Pushcart Prize nominations. He lives in Pittsburgh, where he is the cofounder of the independent literary press Braddock Avenue Books.